# When Aliens Weep

## Species Intervention #6609

By

## J. K. Accinni

## E. K. Publishing
## Lakewood Ranch, Florida

WHEN ALIENS WEEP
SPECIES INTERVENTION #6609
J.K. Accinni

An EK Publishing book published in arrangement with the author, Lakewood Ranch, FL.

Copyright © 2014 J.K. Accinni
Editing by LionheART Publishing House

ISBN: 978-0-9899769-7-8

## Other Books by J.K. Accinni:

Baby (Species Intervention #6609, Book 1)

Echo (Species Intervention #6609, Book 2)

Armageddon Cometh (Species Intervention #6609, Book 3)

Hive (Species Intervention #6609 Book 4)

Evil Among Us (Species Intervention #6609, Book 5)

The One (Species Intervention #6609, Book 6)

Alien Species Intervention Books 1-3

# Earth—Eleven Hours before the End

# Chapter 1

Seth lay prostrate in the dust of the red earth, snot from his exhausted crying jag dried on his face and congealed in the dirt.

It had been hours since the golden creatures and their flying entourage had left with the infernal dog. He'd miserably failed to recover from the shock of his glorious crumbled dreams and fallen asleep while the detritus of his fallen comrades mocked him with the unexplainable evidence of their rag-festooned skeletons.

The clicking sound of a beast slowly awakened him; a foreign noise that penetrated his consciousness, a dark awareness blossoming like a macabre pustule, throbbing and ready to burst its bacterial poisons.

Pain radiated from his clawed hand that lay jammed uncomfortably under his body, screaming for release. Slow to open his gummy eyes, he felt the hot breath of an ursine beast at his neck, forcing him to freeze as it investigated the stench that clung to him; the myriad of odors enticing to the bear, even as the siren call of the Hive tugged at it like a magnet.

The bear clawed once, turning Seth over and forcing him to look straight into the curious face, its breath smelling of berries and grubs. Finding the pull of the Hive irresistible, the bear chuffed in his face then wandered off down the road, leaving Seth to his ignoble fate.

And what a miserable fate that was. He curled into a fetal position, unwilling to lay eyes on what was left of his lover and his men. Their fatal images had been burned indelibly in his mind as they'd taken their last breaths and collapsed in the dirt, the miniscule black and red projectiles returning to the split antlers of the evil and vicious creature known as Echo. *Has that creature enslaved the Others with its diabolical power?* he wondered.

1

Tired of self-pity and with no appreciative audience, Seth began to take stock. The effort expended to force himself into a sitting position wore him down. No matter how hard he tried, his strength ebbed from the emotional distress his efforts were causing. Try as he might, he continued to flounder, unable to invent a plausible way to spin this hideous outcome to his grandiose plans.

The last thing he wanted was to become a laughing stock instead of the conquering hero he'd originally intended. Pathetically, the realization was just sinking in that the only thing conquered was him and his band of misfits and toadies.

He'd been made to look like a fool by two oversized *flying cats . . . no, deer . . . no . . . well, whatever the fuck they are . . .*

*The next time I see those abominations, I'll show them just who they're toying with. If they hadn't caught me off guard . . .*

Seth wiped the traces of his blubbering off his face with the ragged end of his sleeve. He scrambled to his feet and listened for sounds, the pre-dawn wrapping him in its silent awaiting. The absence of further rustlings from the edge of the road told him it must be safe to start his journey back to the tribe's settlement. Alone . . .

Every time he remembered he was on his own, depression returned. How would he explain the loss of his men? He remembered the confused reaction of the tribe as he and his men returned victoriously from the first meeting with the Others, waving Lorna's severed hand and declaring himself the new leader. The quiet covert whispers and tight faces of the women had not escaped his notice. *Who knows what havoc the nasties were working on behind my back while I bravely set out to negotiate with the Others? I did all this for them, the ungrateful bitches.*

Hitching up his pants, Seth stretched, his aching limbs testifying to the many hours he'd lain sleeping on the ground. Turning his back on what was left of his men, he began the long hike back to the settlement, watching as the moon began to disappear, soon to be rendered invisible by the sun's infant rays greedy to claim their rightful turn in the sky.

\*\*\*

Hours later, the dawn long vanished, he knew he neared the tribe. His heartbeat ratcheted up with stress. Every possible lie long discarded, he knew it was time to face the music.

As he ascended the last rise, smoke from multiple breakfast fires rose to greet the late morning sun. From his vantage point, he saw various tribesmen and women still scurrying around with the chores of the morning. Carefree children were chasing each other while older teenagers egged them on.

The ramshackle nature of their dwellings appeared pleasantly blurred from his position, allowing the settlement to take on the appearance of an actual village. In the distance he could see the groves of fruit and nut trees they'd painstakingly transplanted from deep in the mine, a monumental task. The seedlings had thrived in the open under the watchful glare of the sun and the now skilled farming members of the tribe.

To the left, he spied figures in the fields, already at work tending their lush vegetable crops. They appeared to grow wherever they found a spot to plant them. The damage done by hungry roving creatures bothered them little.

A couple wandered away from the children toward an outcrop of rocks, closer to his vantage point. Young lovers? As he watched them kiss, he guessed it wouldn't be long before the young girl claimed her man and started a home of her own.

He tore his gaze away from the young lovers, jealousy an emotion that plagued him forcefully, reminding him of all that he no longer had.

It appeared quite clear that the tribe flourished well under the leadership of his dispatched sister. Did they even need him?

He vainly considered turning around and throwing himself on the mercy of the Others rather than face the certain wrath and scorn of his own people. Seth wiped his beaded brow, the sun making him sweat. Crouched with his back to the encampment, absorbed in his own self-pity, he failed to see members of the tribe stop their chores and stand speechless as the late morning air began to sizzle, the sun rising over the eastern horizon blinding them.

Seth's discomfort from the sun began to sink in. But not in time to witness the first of the monumental solar flares that lit the sky, making the forty-five-mile-wide chunk of metallic space debris glow as it fought with the flare to be the first to reach the vulnerable planet.

# Two Hours Before The End

# Chapter 2

Johno directed the keepers with a heavy heart. The men were ever flexible but he could see their broken spirits in the cant of their shoulders and the pain in their eyes.

"No, my friend. You're pulling up plants. We need to rid the field of the weeds. Like this." Johno demonstrated with a quick slash into the red dirt with his shovel, severing the roots and flipping the plant clear of the soil. He bent his timeworn back to retrieve the weed and stuff it into the sling hanging from his back like the other men.

A hand grasped his shoulder. Johno turned to see one of his men shading his other hand over his eyes and looking toward the hill that led to the woods and the path to the Hive. He just caught a glimpse of some of the other survivors disappearing into the trees. What was that glimmer in the air? *If I didn't know better, I'd say that Baby and Echo were back.*

"Boss, I think they were trying to get our attention."

Johno squinted back up at the hill, evidence of the migration to the Hive littering the ground. "Are you sure?"

He turned back to his trusted men. "I'd better see what's happening. I'll go see if I can find Hud, maybe stop by the kitchen and see what Dezi knows. You boys want to take a break? I'll wait and see what Dezi has for us for lunch while I'm at it."

Watching Johno give the hill another quick glance told his men that the concern in Johno's dark expressive African eyes was more for the loss of their beloved Tobi and her herd than anything else.

Johno started his trek out of the fields amidst the uneasy whispers and mumbling of his men as they took refuge under a huge walnut tree. It served as a welcome respite from an unusually hot late morning sun, a grateful balm to their overheated bodies.

Johno hurried, wiping his perspiring brow with a rag, his shirt plastered to his sleek knotted muscles even as sweat continued to pour down his underarms. He felt an uncoiling in the pit of his stomach, a viper he tried to quell with sheer willpower.

He tried unsuccessfully to shake off his emotional paralysis, served to him by the realization that he no longer shared the planet with the creatures he loved with every fiber of his being. Elephant-tender no more, he would tend crops until, by the grace of the Womb, Tobi and her herd would be allowed to return home. He nurtured the tiny flare of hope, refusing to relinquish his fiercely held aspiration.

Reaching the edge of the field, he raced to the kitchen. From his left, he could see Hud and Ginger Mae at the base of the road leading to the woods.

"Hey there, Hud . . . Ginger Mae. Wait up!"

The couple turned and waited, the smiles on their welcoming faces slowly melting as Johno's dripping condition and obvious state caused them to tense.

Johno caught up, heaving breath cutting off his words. "Hey . . . ah . . . You guys . . . you guys see anything unusual?"

"Like what, Johno? Something wrong?" They eyed him with concern.

Johno gulped a deep breath, calming down. "We thought we saw something on the hill. It looked like Echo or Baby to me . . . I'm not sure." He stared at the large box that hung from Hud's side. "Where are you going with that, my friend?"

Ginger Mae tugged on Hud's arm. "We need to get going, Hud, no telling how long we're going to have access to the Hive. Johno, we have no idea what you're talking about. You want to come with us? We could use some help." Turning, she waved at Peter returning to the kitchen, motioning for him to join them. Jogging up to the base of the hill, he asked. "What's up, guys?"

"Johno thinks he saw Baby and Echo on the hill."

Johno raised his hand, "No, not on the hill . . . at the top. My men thought they saw Cobby and Bonnie."

Peter screwed up his face. "No, not Bonnie. She's in the kitchen.

6

I'm on my way there now."

"Can you spare another half hour or so?" Hud asked.

"Yeah," interjected Ginger Mae. "We could use the extra hand to carry some of the last of the good stuff from storage. I know it'll be needed eventually. Why waste it?" She turned her charm on Peter. "Please . . . Bonnie won't mind waiting with the babies."

He dismissed Johno's concerns, "Wish we could help you." Looping her arm through Hud and Peter's, she proceeded to tug them up the hill.

Peter cranked his sweaty neck back to Johno. "Can you stop by the kitchen, Johno? Let Bonnie know?"

"Sure. You guys go on. I'm headed for the kitchen anyway, got to feed the crew. You be off now. Keep your eyes open." He waved at the chummy threesome but they'd already turned their backs to him, deep in conversation, their laughter carrying back down the hill.

Johno watched quietly, his wise eyes scanning the quiet woods. Ginger Mae's voice was now a distant musical note fleeting and fading as they moved among the trees. The viper in his stomach twitched a warning. *Yeah, yeah, I hear you, my friend. Please . . . just settle down for me. I pray you're wrong and it's just my imagination.*

Johno hurriedly made his way back to the kitchen, Crystal now weighing heavily on his mind. He needed to find her and get her up to the Hive. Just on the off-chance that the viper in his stomach was correct.

Rounding the side of the kitchen, he observed the door closing behind someone. He heard voices inside as the door swung back open to admit him.

"Johno, what are you doing here?" Crystal approached her husband to give him a resounding kiss then turned back to the other survivors, who watched with stupefied faces.

Clyde, Salina and Jennifer stood examining the empty kitchen; there was no sign of Dezi or the lunch fixings that would normally be apparent. Dezi's counters sparkled clean and clear. Not a crumb in sight.

Clyde escorted his two women to a table, leaning in to be extra solicitous toward Jennifer who had yet to recover fully from her mental breakdown suffered the night they'd met the members of the tribe from the Franklin Mines. It was forbidden to mention the names Lorna and Seth around her even as Lorna's revelation about her parentage brought great bittersweet joy to them all. All the survivors had great hopes for the future and the uniting of Lorna's tribe with their group.

Father Garcia and Maddy approached from the confines of the nursery, worried expressions now shared by all.

"I don't understand. Where are the babies? Where's Cobby? And Chloe? They were here when we left." The blank looks on everyone's faces told Johno everything he feared.

"We need to leave now." All traces of the wise man they loved now vanished as Johno's face sagged, looking chalky and threatening panic.

From their table, Clyde's voice boomed out. "Settle down, everyone. Salina, why don't you go rustle up some grub? Dezi won't mind." He slapped her on the rump as she rose to obey. "You can still cook up some fine vittles, can't you?"

She gave him a quick glance of annoyance. "Try that again and the only vittles I cook up will be the ones I rip from your big belly." Salina huffed her way to Dezi's kitchen and grabbed some bowls amid the laughter from Father Garcia and Maddy.

"No, no . . . you don't understand. Something's going to happen. Something *bad*. That's why the kitchen's empty. We thought we saw them on the hill to the Hive. My men thought they were trying to get our attention. We need to *run*. Now!"

Clyde stood with his hand raised. "Now just a gosh darn minute."

Johno shook his head sadly and grabbed Crystal's hand. "Good luck, everyone." He dragged her out the door.

Ginger Mae stood with her husband and Peter in the old supply room surveying the shambles left from their effort to salvage what they could. The beam of her flashlight lit up what was left: long discarded shelves broken by the Kreyven when it had brought the contents of a department store to the Hive in preparation for their arrival so many decades ago.

"I think I saw the box of penlights under that junk." Ginger Mae lifted a piece of metal off a smashed box.

Hud hurried to her side. "Let us handle that, hon. If you're right, we could sure use some more light right now."

Peter knelt at the other end of the pile. "I wonder when the membranes disappeared. It never occurred to me that we'd no longer be able to see in here."

"Do you think they'll just leave what's at the mouth of the Hive and in the big cavern?' Ginger Mae asked.

"I don't think so, hon. Wil said it's the Kreyven's job to secure the Hive. They can't have anyone accidentally getting into the portal. They'd never find their way back. Even though there are now only two paths, one to Oolaha and one to . . . hmmm . . . I don't think he told me. I wonder where the other path goes to? Oh well . . . doesn't matter now. We better just concentrate on grabbing anything useful that's left and get out of here."

The threesome went to work, Ginger Mae with her flashlight and the men with the tiny pocket lights. It didn't take long to fill their big box. Hud managed to find a pile of work boots sitting on a heap of fabric as if someone else had readied them and promptly left them behind. Ginger Mae found a small cookbook in the rubble and slipped it into her pocket to hand over to Dezi. She was pleased with the tiny treat she could take to surprise him.

"I think we'd better head back now, Hud. The box is full."

Hud bent over to heft the box onto his broad shoulders. "Wait, what about some of this broken metal shelving? We could find a handy use for this someday. We might be grateful we grabbed some of it while we had the chance."

Ginger Mae bent down to gather it in her arms. She glanced up to see Hud heaving the box. "Come on, Peter. Gather some of this up with me. It's too heavy for me to carry more than a couple pieces by myself."

"Let me tie a few pieces together for you. Hand me that twine. It'll be easier to carry that way." After tying two bunches of the metal together, Peter slipped one bundle under Ginger Mae's arms. "How's that feel?"

Ginger Mae gave it a test. "Good. Not too heavy."

Hud nodded in their direction. "We gotta move. Peter, can you tuck in the tail of that twine? I don't want her to trip on it."

Peter wrapped the tail of the twine around her hand, securing it tightly then bent to do the same for his bunch. "Okay. We're set."

The three of them headed back down the lonely winding corridors, the shuffle of their feet on the rock floor the only sound as they conserved their strength for their burdens. Ginger Mae took the lead since she still carried the only flashlight, tucked into her breast pocket and sending most of the light straight up. Still, it was enough. She honestly thought she could traverse the corridors blindfolded anyway.

Before long, they arrived in the main cavern; the cavern of hellos and goodbyes, wedding and funerals, joy and sadness. Setting down her burden, she complained, "I need a rest, Hud. This thing is killing my arm."

The men halted, Peter moving over to Ginger Mae to examine the twine wrapped around her wrist. "Too tight?" he asked.

"Yeah, but I don't want to redo it now. Let's just get out of here." She bent to pick up the metal rods again. The beam of her flashlight moved with her, now focused on the cavern wall near the portal.

"Wait," Hud commanded. Setting down his heavy box, he walked to the wall. "Ginger Mae, can you train the light back over here?" With her free hand she removed the flashlight from her pocket to illuminate the wall.

Hud ran his hand over the wall. *The membrane was gone.*

"It looks like the portal has closed too." Peter's voice trembled.

"Wow, we really *are* alone now. Hud? Come on. I just want to get out of here.' Ginger Mae sniffed while Hud turned his back to the wall and hoisted his box.

"Okay, babe. I hear you. Let's go see what Dezi's cooking up for lun—"

With a terrific rendering, the wall exploded and the Kreyven burst into the cavern, lighting it up with its flashing iridescent streaks of illumination. It descended down on Hud, crashing his box to the rock floor. Ginger Mae screamed as her husband was sucked into the gelatinous mass without a sound.

10

Before she had a second to finish her scream, the Kreyven was on her, wrapping its sinuous mass around her, metal burden and all.

As Ginger Mae fought with the shock and surprise, she heard Peter scream and felt the beast move, carrying them along with it.

*Hud, where's Hud?* She found she was unable to speak as she felt an unfamiliar constriction at the same time as her light dropped from her hand and she was engulfed in a moving darkness.

Johno and Crystal ran through the woods. If Crystal stumbled, he simply yanked her back on her feet and ignored her protests. The heat from the sun intensified, drenching them thoroughly with their sweat. The urgency of their run forced them to look ahead and miss the dynamics of the solar flares headed to Earth and illuminating the gargantuan metal chunk of meteor that engulfed the sky from the west.

The comforting granite rock that marked the entrance to their salvation loomed in his eyesight, but he didn't slow down. The safety of the Hive lay yards away. Finally, plunging into the cooler darkness, he let Crystal catch her breath, his anxiety slowly abating.

"We made it, my love." He held his wife close, searching for moisture to loosen his parched and gummy tongue from the roof of his mouth. For once in her life, Crystal kept her smart mouth closed; only gently begging him to explain.

"Johnny . . . please. What in tarnation's going on?" Her brows knitted into a furrow.

"Not now, Crystal." He held her tightly in his arms, averting his terror-filled face. The viper in his stomach uncurled as his senses shrieked that his ordeal was not over. "I think . . . I think we need to keep moving."

They stumbled on, the darkness their friend as its slight coolness revived them. Johno moved on, the cavern of the portal dead ahead.

As they plunged into the cavern, they heard a muffled scream. Staring ahead, they were greeted by the stunning sight of the Kreyven in all its iridescent glory. Before they had a chance to call out, it plummeted into the rock wall to disappear, plunging them back into darkness.

Like zombies in a frenzy, the pair rushed to the cavern wall. Crystal tripped over Hud's fallen box, dumping the scavenged treasures. She bent down, her searching fingers discovering the tiny penlights. When she clicked one on, she was met with the sight of her husband pounding on the solid rock wall; there was no membrane, no portal . . . just unbroken rock. Tears flowed down his ebony face, freezing her to the spot.

"*Quick*, woman. Bring that light here." His fingers moved more frantically, nails splitting and bleeding. "We need to find it, Crystal. *Help me.*"

She rushed to her husband's side in a daze. Her stalwart rock, her love, the calmest man she had ever known . . . was ungluing in front of her eyes.

It was their good fortune that, when the blast came, the shockwave swept through the tunnels of the Hive, blowing them apart with such force that Johno and Crystal never knew what hit them.

Ginger Mae felt herself surrounded and compressed by the undulating mass of the Kreyven; the motion much like the beating of a giant heart. She tried to remove the twine from her hand but it now dug painfully into her skin and she couldn't locate the end that Peter had so carefully tucked away.

Instead, she wrapped herself around her metal bundle, hoping to stabilize herself. Her senses registered a strange pull exerting pressure on her body.

She tried to scream but to no avail. Where were Hud and Peter? *Please save me now, Hud, I need you so.* She felt herself moving through the mass of the Kreyven, its constrictions slowing her movement but not stopping it. She felt safe with the Kreyven, absorbing a calmness from the beast yet unable to negate her growing panic from her slipping-away sensation. She scrambled to hold on to something; her hands and feet unable to find purchase. Instinctively she knew she must stay with the Kreyven. It would take her to Hud. *It's in the service of the Womb, isn't it? Perhaps it's been sent by Netty or Daisy to take us somewhere.*

The darkness burst suddenly with agonizing light as she was pulled free of the comforting embrace of the Kreyven. She clung tightly to her metal bundle as she felt herself in a freefall, the pulling sensation growing stronger. She landed with a hard crash after what felt like an eternity, the light still blinding and her captive wrist now in pain so intense that she fainted.

# Oolaha

# Day One AE (After Earth)

# Chapter 3

The survivors stared as Kenya marched up to Kane and ripped the Good Book from his hands. Shaking it in her fists, her fingers trembling with anger, she lashed out.

"*This* book . . . of *all* books? Why are you even reading it? It should be called *The Great Lie*. If we'd known the truth, we would still be on Earth." Bitter tears flowed from her desolate eyes as she threw imploring looks to them all.

"I don't want to be here. I want my baby to have a home. I want to be part of my community. I want Kane to go to work and come home to help me change diapers and eat my lousy dinner and tell me he loves it. I want a normal life. No more monsters, no more things that fly and read my mind, no more secrets and surprises. If I find out someone is holding out on us again . . . believe me, chickey, you ain't *never* seen the kind of hell I'm gonna raise . . ." Kenya's voice tailed off into a pitiful squeak. She tossed the offending Bible to the side where it landed in a heap, forlornly discarded.

Kane took her in his arms and her sobbing increased. "I just want to go home," she blubbered. "They don't really want us here anyway. We're nothing to this Womb thing. I don't want to be an *accommodation*."

Abby piped up, Chloe's strength beginning to flag. "It'll be okay, Kenya. Just hold on until we get settled in before you freak out. We need to get Chloe some care and check on the babies. At least we're alive and safe. I'm sure we'd all like to have a breakdown, but I don't think any of us have that kind of energy to waste. I know I don't. We can deal with our past later. Right now we'd better concentrate on the here and now." She panned the crowd with her golden eyes, assessing their blood-drained complexions, heavy with deeply etched loss and grief.

"Please . . . Netty . . . can you just get us to where we need to go . . . ?"

Netty opened her mouth to speak when the Kreyven suddenly burst from the dome and portal where it had disappeared. The survivors shrank back as the Kreyven moved toward them, its mass sending its telltale stench of ozone before it.

Kenya clenched Kane in a death grip. "Oh no . . . not more, please . . ."

The Kreyven stopped before them, the gelatinous mass rippling with striating flashes of light and a bulge deep in what appeared to be its throat. From high up, it lowered its head, the bulge moving forward to be vomited onto the ground.

A collective gasp from the crowd failed to wake an unconscious Hud. Seconds ticked by as the Kreyven hovered over the survivors, then hastened off to the distant dwellings, their fairy-tale colors advertising the survivors' eventual destination.

Bonnie was the first to break the silence, her face radiant with hope. Excited, she rushed to Hud's side, announcing to the crowd, "We're *all* saved. The Kreyven came to the rescue again." Her head swiveled back to follow the path of the Kreyven's retreat as she knelt on the ground to take Hud's hand. "Where's it going? Where's Peter? *Where's my husband?*" she shrieked.

Revolting sounds of vomiting drew their attention back to Hud, and Daisy knelt to join Bonnie. Hud threw off their hands as he rolled to the side, vomiting again.

A tiny robot cleaner emerged from the dome, this one on flat legs that slid over the grass on which Hud lay. He stared bleary-eyed at the strange sight of the creature as it cleaned the mess he'd left in the grass. As if sensing Hud's scrutiny, the creature cocked its head and leaned forward toward Hud. It gave him a thorough once-over with its minion-like eyes before retreating back into the dome.

Hud coughed and wiped his mouth with the back of his hand.

Daisy slipped her small hand back into Hud's, her voice betraying her emotion. "Where's Mom, Hud?"

"And Peter? Did he come with you?" asked Bonnie's quavering voice.

Wil stepped forward to pull the women away. He whispered gently into their confused and hopeful faces. "Give him a few minutes, ladies . . . please."

Hud gratefully nodded his head in Wil's direction and cleared his throat. "I sure am happy to see you guys." He looked around. "Peter and Ginger Mae aren't here. Where are we?" He looked through the legs crowded around him to catch glimpses of the milling wildlife and the thousands of minions that vibrated in the air above their heads like an upside-down sea of golden shimmering waves. He tore his eyes from the improbable sight above and looked back to Wil, a dawning of truth written all over him.

"Oolaha? We're on Oolaha?"

Wil carefully nodded his head. "Yes, Hud. The others were warned by Baby and Echo in time to save themselves. We have no idea how many were saved. You're the only one we've seen emerge from a portal since Cobby arrived with Chloe, Kenya, Kane, Dezi and Bonnie. And the babies." He pointed to the now closed portal in their dome. "The Kreyven sealed this portal off a while ago. We thought we were the last ones. How did you wind up in the portal over there?" He pointed to the other dome in the distance.

"I . . . I don't know," he said haltingly. "We were in the storage room and heading back to the settlement with a few things when the Kreyven burst through the wall and grabbed us."

"Us? Who is *us,* Hud? Tell me . . . tell me," Bonnie beseeched.

His fingers to the bridge of his nose, Hud massaged slowly. "Ah . . . well . . . Ginger Mae of course. And Peter."

Grateful tears slid down Bonnie's face. She threw herself at Hud, clasping him in a desperate embrace. "Oh Lord. Thank you, Hud. Thank you . . ."

Hud extricated himself from her grasp. "But where are they?" he demanded.

Bonnie sat up with a startled blink. "You don't *know?*" she asked.

Wil shook his head, his wings drooping in sympathy. "They aren't here, Hud."

Silence hung over the crowd. The only sounds were the fluttering of wings, the restless milling of elephants, and the collective sobbing heartbreak of the survivors as they realized their unrelenting pain had no limits.

It wasn't the pain that woke Ginger Mae. It was the cold and the smell. Even though she could feel herself shiver, her nose told her something burned nearby.

She had no idea how long she'd been out, but the hot-poker pain and swelling from her wrist told her it was broken.

Glancing out of the corner of her eye, she was confronted with a filmy image of an empty room. *How can this be?* She shook her head to clear her eyes, setting off a firestorm in her head. Her eyes squinted and blinked but she was unable to clear her vision. A burning sensation in her eyes told her something was wrong.

"Ugh." Ginger Mae stopped moving to assess her situation and relieve her headache. Even if she couldn't see clearly, she knew she lay on her back on a hard floor. She slowly scrunched her body together into a fetal position as her stomach boiled, threatening to erupt. "Ugh." Her mouth tasted like metal and a sensation of grease clung to the air, further exacerbating her rebelling stomach.

A new sound pierced her consciousness. A buzzing. Like a thousand crickets firing over one another.

Vomiting onto the floor, she heard a different sound. A prickling gave her hope she wasn't alone.

Choking through the vomit she called out, "Hello? Hello? *Anybody there?*"

Suddenly, the burning smell intensified. Wiping her hand across her mouth, she shrank back as two shapes materialized and weaved their way toward her. Ginger Mae blinked hard, her vision stubbornly refusing to clear.

"Hello? Who are you? Where am I?" The figures hovered over her. She felt something on her neck and all went black.

Ginger Mae awoke strapped to a hard surface. No matter how hard she twisted, she felt trapped. She could feel her metal burden had been removed, but her broken wrist felt weighed down with a brick. At least the pain had abated.

Blinking furiously, she tried desperately to clear her sight. As she gave up, her eyes were finally able to make out a shadowy object that appeared to be throwing off sparks, the tiny lights rising and falling like a delicate waterfall . . . disappearing with the limitations of her vision. She had no way to gauge how close it was; her vision was now almost useless.

She sniffed the air, redolent of the same hot burning smell from her room. Rocking her head back and forth, she felt obstacles on each side of her head. Softly rubbing her head against one, she discovered hard metal with only a tiny clearance between it and her body. Her fight or flight reflex paralyzed her with fear. The sound of her rushing blood flooded her ears.

The burning smell became more intense. Ginger Mae started with panic as strange, nebulous figures hovered over her helpless body, the sparkling waterfalls becoming clearer. Her terror rocketed through the roof as the metal alongside her head snapped and clamped down on her forehead. She was fully immobile, only her eyelids dancing with anxiety as she continued to try to clear her sight.

Thankfully for Ginger Mae, as one of the hovering figures reached behind her neck, the dark came rushing in like a long-lost lover, embracing her with its own benign anesthetic to which she gratefully surrendered.

Ginger Mae regained consciousness slowly, the darkness threatening to overwhelm her with its perilous mystery. She realized the hard floor of her enclosure had been softened by a pad of some sort on which she lay. Trying to reach up to her face, she found the weight on her wrist still oppressed her. Her tongue stuck to the roof of her mouth, swollen and dry along with her throat. She knew she must have water soon. Her stomach growled with a fervor that caused her to question how long she'd been out.

She fumbled around, raising her good arm to her face and discovered an obstruction covering her eyes.

"Oh . . . erm . . ." Her tongue floundered; a feeble lump in her mouth. She patted the obstruction down then tried to find some slack to gain purchase with which to rip it off. The material clung to her like plastic; there wasn't a single seam or slack spot to give her a chance to slip a finger under. Her fright increased as she realized she must be a captive somewhere and was clearly not alone. But where was she? And where were Hud and Peter?

Her fear so paralyzed her that she couldn't call out, even if she'd been able to make her useless tongue function. She tried to swallow; her mouth was parched and her throat raw and abused.

The helplessness of her situation hit her like a locomotive. Who had put the infernal blockage over her eyes and why? What didn't they want her to see? *I need information and now.* Rocking her body to and fro, she found no aches and pains. The nausea she remembered upon her first awakening was gone, *thank the Womb. Womb . . . now where the heck did that come from?*

Reaching out with her good arm, she felt around the floor of her enclosure, smashing her hand against something hard that tipped over and leaked moisture over her arm. She raised her arm to her nose and sniffed. She tentatively brought it to her mouth and sucked. *Water.* At least she thought it was water but then realized it had a chalky aftertaste.

Scrambling as best as she could, she maneuvered her body over to the spot where the spilt water lay on the floor. She powered through a wave of dizziness and managed to lower her mouth to the floor to lap up the remaining moisture.

Convulsively, she searched for the container with her good arm. In her scramble to get to the water, it must have rolled away. The longer her questing hand roamed over the floor, the more frightened she became. Locating the water container had become a representation of control. She *must* regain a semblance of control if she was going to survive this. She tried to push away the thought of breaking down completely. She could feel tears slipping from her bound eyes.

Suddenly exhausted, she rolled back to her pad and huddled, her tears now coming in sobs that soaked into the obstruction across her eyes.

Not being able to tell if her eyelids were open or closed was maddening. Overwhelmed with worry about Hud and Peter, she fell into an exhausted sleep, only to be awakened by a pervasive burning smell that signaled terror.

She feigned sleep as the smell became stronger. She thought she heard a yelp but, as she strained to hear more, the only sound she identified was the sound of bees buzzing; louder then softer, rising in pitch then fading.

She froze at the sound of something being dragged across the floor. She felt it pass in front of her then stop. She heard no more as the buzzing of bees faded in the distance, and then she was left again in complete silence.

As her heart continued its frenetic beating, she took a deep breath, hoping it would slow her respiration to a more normal level. Absently, she ran her hands through her hair. *What the . . . ?* Perplexed over a strange sensation, she withdrew her hand. Shaking it to rid herself of the softness that had clung to her fingers, she was unable to see the clumps of her hair as they fell from her scalp and fingers to land in her lap like spent tufts of gossamer.

*What the heck was that?* Gathering courage, she reached up to her face again and ran her hand over her head, swatting at imaginary bugs. Finding nothing in the air around her head, she relaxed, breathing in relief as more of her hair silently detached from her head to lie unseen about her shoulders.

The minutes ticked by. Before long they piled up as hours. Ginger Mae's stomach ached with a relentless acknowledgment of hunger and thirst. Her psyche begged for the darkness to go away. She needed light. It was only in the light that she could begin her hunt for *. . . for . . . for what?* she wondered. Her mind searched, confusion wearing her down. *I have to find it.* It was only then that she could begin to figure out how to get back home. She didn't know where she was but she knew instinctively that this wasn't her beloved Earth. *But what? What do I need to find?*

Before long, her tears stopped. Her strength taxed to its limits, she slept.

*Crash—* Ginger Mae snapped out of her sleep and sat up. *What was that?* Sniffing the air, she recognized the unmistakable dreaded burning smell. Huddled tightly on her pad she drew herself into a ball, hoping to be overlooked, if only she could make herself small enough.

She strained her ears, desperate to catch the sound of something familiar. She sensed the presence of others: movements and a thump. The darkness pressed in on her. She clamped her hand over her mouth to prevent herself from screaming out in fear. The sounds stopped as suddenly as they'd begun, the burning smell receding. The darkness froze her in place as her tears welled up again.

From out of the silence and the darkness, she heard a scrape.

"Hello," she ventured, her voice timid and tremulous. She was greeted by nothing more than silence. "Is anyone there?" The silence slapped her in the face again. Frightened yet mollified, she curled back into a ball to return to sleep. Who knew what trouble the singular sound would bring her? Maybe it was just her imagination or wishful thinking. Her mind eventually switched off to suck her deeper into the blackness.

The black void now her constant companion, her only escape became sleep: The sleep of the innocent that promised temporary oblivion yet insidiously and unknowingly robbed her of her memory. For it was during her sleep that the residue of the minute toxic substance contained in the hot burning smell—the odor that terrorized her so—was fractionally destroying the cells in her brain. In the part of the brain that stored memory; the essence of who we are and who Ginger Mae had been.

# Chapter 4

The tired survivors trudged pitifully toward the huge, shimmering city. Thousands of creatures fluttered above their heads; golden minions and hundreds of their white, curly-haired vulpine nooglets.

From time to time, a minion would dart to the ground to reach out and touch one of the survivors, forcing Baby or Echo to dart forward and silently warn them off.

Stunned and preoccupied with their grief, the survivors trudged on like punch-drunken zombies of the popular and historic bygone golden age of twenty-first-century Earth's literature.

Baby, Netty and Wil guided them toward the city. Sticking like glue to Barney and Chloe, Echo spoke to all that welcomed her into their frightened and grieving minds. Her shimmering thoughts swirled brighter and brighter.

"We have much we must do, my Sister and Brothers. The Womb is not pleased you are here but again, accommodations will be made. I am happy to be able to join my long lost brother and sister minions at last. I have much to do myself. A feast is being prepared for you in your private quarters. There will be time to present you officially to our population later. We will be allowed time to grieve and you can acclimate yourself before your jobs are assigned."

Some of the survivors began to mutter. Bonnie stopped dead in her tracks.

"Work? What do you mean, Echo? *We can't work*. We need to find out where my husband is." Agitated, she turned to the small crowd, her eyes resting on Hud. "And Ginger Mae . . . we need to find them, right, Hud?" The strain of hysteria in her voice was pronounced. Hud rushed to her side. He held her in his arms.

"Damn straight, Bonnie." Over her head, he searched the faces of his fellow survivors. Wil stepped toward them.

"Of course, my friends. We will do everything we can to find Peter and Ginger Mae. Echo was just thinking ahead. No one will push you until you are ready but we all have long lives ahead of us and we must plan."

Bonnie struggled in Hud's arms, her face blotchy from tears, and a flash of anger surfaced. "It's bad enough I just lost my mother. But my life is over without my husband . . . don't you understand? " Breaking free of Hud, she stood before Wil, gesticulating wildly. "I need to see the Womb. *Let me see him.*" She grabbed on to Wil's arm as Hud and Abby rushed to calm her.

Eluding them, she threw herself at Netty. Grabbing the alluring Elder by her shoulders, Bonnie shook her hard.

"I know you can fix this. Let me speak to the Womb. Let me speak to him . . . *now!*" Bonnie screamed her frustrations and broken heart at Netty, who stood stoically until the distraught woman burned down, reduced to sobs.

Bonnie finally slid down the length of Netty's figure to collapse on the ground. Tears of sympathy from the other survivors didn't help. Dezi stooped down to Bonnie as her sobs changed to hiccups. He pulled a dishrag from his apron, extending it to help her dry her face. Bonnie just stared at the rag, her face a mask of hopelessness. They stared into one another's anguished eyes while the other survivors held their breath.

"Hud, give me a hand." Dezi and Hud struggled, trying to bring Bonnie to her feet. Her hold on her emotional state collapsed along with her body. Taking hold again, Hud lifted her in his strong arms, his face set and grim.

"Okay, Wil. Please . . . let's just get to where we need to go."

Silently, the group trudged on, the clatter of their airborne entourage soon joined by the worrisome trumpet of Tobi as she left her herd to dash forward as soon as she realized Hud was carrying Bonnie.

The group parted to let the worried pachyderm approach Hud. Tobi's trunk roamed over Bonnie's limp body. She listened for Bonnie's heart and the sounds that would show her lungs still drew breath. Soft rumbles from deep within Tobi's huge bulk marked her concern.

Taking wing, Echo left Barney to alight atop Tobi's back where she proceeded to relax the matriarch and prod her back to her herd. Rejoining the survivors, Echo's swirling projections urged the group on toward the city that now rose high up over them.

As the survivors got closer, the pastel effect diminished, fading into an iridescent glow. They stood transfixed. Cobby spoke for all of them.

"What the heck *is* this?"

For the city resembled a colossal beating heart, clearly alive. Its walls were made of a clear organic substance riddled with giant pathways throbbing with life and resembling the same veins and arteries contained in their own bodies. Though they contained something quite different than blood; something that gave the luminous iridescent quality to the minions and the Elders.

Chloe spoke up, her arms still wrapped around Jose and Abby. "I know how you all feel. But we have nothing to fear. This is merely the most visible manifestation of the Womb."

"This is the *Womb?*" Hud asked.

Chloe nodded as the rest of the survivors allowed their revulsion to speak for itself.

"Ah . . . Netty . . . do you mind explaining why we need to go inside this . . . this . . . ah . . ." Dezi's voice evinced a note of panic.

Netty raised her hands in a gesture of supplication. "Please . . . it's alright. This is just the framework the minions must work in. *Yes,* it is alive. The minions plug into the Womb for guidance. Much as Baby and Echo plugged into the membrane in the Hive. This is the communication pathway for the minions. It also provides sustenance for those not able to *eat* from the power of their sun due to their duties."

Netty met the eyes of the survivors, as comprehension and wonder replaced the fear in their countenance.

"The minions don't require shelter from the elements on this planet. There are no weather patterns as we know them. This planet revolves around their sun star in such an orbit that the entire planet is stable and stays temperate. It is always at the same distance from the sun, a feat matched nowhere else in any galaxy I know of. The bodies of water are all salt-free and emanate from below—the water table is very shallow. This planet serves as a staging area for their missions. Look." Netty pointed to the membrane where shadowy figures could be seen scurrying around in service to any number of mysterious projects.

"Not there . . . over there." Netty directed them to the right of the organic entrance to the Womb. Everyone could plainly see a portion of the Womb that appeared darker, less transparent.

"That's where we're going. It's for us. That's where we will live. Some of us will work there." She glanced at Dezi. "I'm thinking your kitchen will need to be expanded in there. When Wil and I were in attendance, we never needed much of a facility." She nodded to the crowd. "I think it's time to fashion something more permanent." She smiled at Dezi, "Whatever you feel you need is available with the help of the Kreyven. If we're lucky, we'll get the assistance of the one most familiar with humans. We may not be able to match everything you are comfortable with from Earth but we can come darn close."

"What do you mean, Netty? You mean there are more Kreyvens?" Kane's eyes widened at the prospect.

Netty glanced at him with amusement. "Of course there are. Did you think an asset as valuable as the Kreyven would be expended to save a few human lives if there were only one? The Womb has galaxies and galaxies to monitor. Other interventions are occurring as we speak." Turning away, she laughed. "You may never see more than one Kreyven at a time. They are the busiest life form ever produced by the Womb."

As the survivors' attention turned back to the minion city they advanced their inspection, awed by the walls of the Womb that extended forty to sixty feet in the air, structured in various configurations. Not a single square corner was observed; roundness abounded, yet it appeared sturdy. An almost imperceptible motion vibrated the entire structure, its rhythm clearly a result of the iridescent fluid being pumped through the veins and arteries. But pumped to where?

Cobby stepped up to the structure, testing the outer wall. All could see the slight give, showing the pliant nature of the Womb.

"Do not fear, Captain. It is quite indestructible."

"It's not that, Netty . . . I'm just a bit queasy with the thought I'll be living inside this . . . this . . . organ."

"On the contrary, Captain. You will be living inside the Womb. There is no place as wondrous anywhere in all the galaxies."

From behind them, they suddenly heard what could be taken as a warning siren; staccato beeps, not unpleasant but clear in their universal message. Their hovering entourage immediately pulled higher into the sky. Wil and Netty directed them all to the side, clearing away from the huge Womb opening to watch as a hurried group of minions came into view.

They looked much the same as Baby and Echo except for one. It was perched astride a huge mobile sphere that appeared to be floating across the grass plain with only the minion's golden leather touch.

"It conceals a gravitational device, very much the same one the Kreyven utilizes in its work," Wil explained in a hushed tone. "This type of sphere is only used when there has been a cull."

The minion sitting astride glanced their way, the most magnificent flaming butterfly attached to one antler.

"Wow, get a loada that," Kenya remarked. "I want me one a *them*." Even with the sun not fully set, the butterfly trailed sparks that danced in a slow loop behind the minion—the only one that had such a magnificent creature attached.

The survivors' collective awe sang as the sphere moved closer, the minion aboard intently interested in them as its radiant eyes rested on the distraught Bonnie, nodding its head at her as they passed, trailing a slight scent of spicy lemon.

Hud spoke up. "What the heck was that about?"

Netty cocked her eye and turned to Baby who sent shimmering swirls into their minds.

"That was a navigator. She is an IV. It is her job to make sure we know the correct path back to Oolaha after a cull. We can't afford to wander into the stream of any of the billions of magnetic trails that hold the cosmos together. They can be quite destructive."

"A cull," someone said from the group. "What's a cull?"

"A cull is when the Womb has decided a danger needs to be

removed. They are brought here to study. If the situation is not rectified, another cull may be instituted. Here at the Womb is where the minions conduct their studies and experiments on the culled life forms."

Faces turned white, confusion abounding.

"Experiments, Baby?" Jose's voice contained an edge. "Is that what you did on Earth? You culled?"

"Of course, Brother Jose. We have culled from Earth for millions of years. We also cull to observe evolution. Sometimes a species is not adapting well. We need to decide if it's worth modifying its DNA to help it survive or let the doomed species fade from existence. But that is a mere curiosity. The most important function is to ensure harmony. In the worse cases, removing the offending species with an intervention most dire is the only solution."

Jose scanned the crowd, his eyebrow raised. "Well, doesn't that just sound ducky, Baby? I think we need to sit down and have a long talk about what happened to Earth and what you minions have been up to. I'm assuming your plans are for Abby and I to be in on the culls?"

"Yes, Brother Jose. There will be much for you to do."

Abby's face reflected surprise and confusion. "Can we table this conversation for now? I don't like where I think it's going and we need to get Bonnie and Chloe some attention."

She waved her hand to include the rest of the survivors. "I'm sure we're all ready to eat and sleep, right, gang?" She appealed to Baby, "I just don't think we can handle any more surprises right now." Murmurs of assent convinced Baby as he turned to escort them into the Womb's embrace.

The group didn't walk far before they were confronted with a barricade.

"For now, everyone is forbidden to enter further into the Womb without an escort," explained Netty. Pointing to the right, an opening appeared in the Womb wall. "This will be your quarters. Please don't wander around outside without the escort of a minion." She smiled. "We wouldn't want you to wander into a portal to another world by mistake."

Netty leaned back, pensively eyeing the hovering entourage. The quick and bright faces of the nooglets and the resident minions showed no lessening of their excitement.

"Baby, can you tell our fan club we will be saying goodnight for now?" The words were no sooner out of her mouth than the curious hovering creatures disappeared over the barricade. Netty turned with a sigh.

"Don't worry, they'll be back tomorrow." Gesturing with her arm she said, "Shall we?"

Taking a last look at the soaring walls of the Womb, the small group entered their new home.

The walls cast iridescent light that enabled all to see even as the natural light from the unfamiliar sun dimmed. The temperature felt a few degrees cooler than they were used to on Earth and a similar organic smell permeated the air. Sniffing discreetly, the survivors all noticed a slight sweeter note that they thought emanated from the walls of the Womb and traces of the spicy lemon that followed the mysterious minion IV with her striking flaming butterfly.

The first room consisted of a large, empty space. The ceilings soared, the light was luminous but that was all. Several smaller spaces funneled off the main entry, bereft of doors.

"Bedrooms." Netty approached an alcove, beckoning for them to follow. Entering the alcove they were confronted with what looked like a blank panel. It consisted of the same organic tissue the walls were made from, and had a large dark circle in the middle. Wil strolled up to the panel, placing his hand flat against it.

"You might have some fun with this for a while. Just place your hand like mine, clear your mind, and visualize any object you think you need. Visualizing its function will help and allow it to be delivered quicker." Wil glanced around. "Anyone want to try it?"

Kane stepped boldly to the console placing his hand flat against the dark circle. He turned to Kenya. "What do you think, babe? A nice comfortable bed?"

Kenya's eyes lit up, her sagging shoulders telegraphing her weariness. "Yeah, and don't forget to ask for pillows."

Kane's face relaxed then formed into a constipated intentness. All were quiet as they awaited the requested bed. Nothing happened. He looked up to Wil in question. Wil grinned back.

"Come with me." They funneled back into the large room where they managed to catch a glimpse of what appeared to be the little sister of the Krevyen in all her rainbow glory as she hastened into a hole that had parted in the Womb's wall. It sealed seamlessly behind her.

"That was a dwelling procurement Kreyven. It will deliver anything within reason."

And deliver it had. Sitting before them was what appeared to be a bed. At least it looked like it could be slept upon. It contained an assortment of pillows, all white. The bed itself was also white. A comforter of sorts lay at its base, also white.

"It's not very inviting," Kenya said, slowly approaching to give it a test for softness. "It looks like a hospital bed."

"I guess I forgot to mention. Kane obviously didn't think of a color. You must be as detailed as possible when requesting supplies. You'll get used to it. Don't be afraid to be creative. If you don't imagine the color of an object, it will be delivered without color." Netty swept her hand toward the bed. "Hence . . . white. Complete absence of color, just as you ordered."

Kenya turned to Kane, glowering. He laughingly backed away, hands held like shields in front of him.

"Don't worry, babe. I promise I'll do better next time." As Kenya and Kane's antics continued, Netty caught Cobby glancing surreptitiously at her. She gave a casual nod and motioned toward the alcove with her head. Leaving Chloe in Jose's care, she casually maneuvered her way back to the alcove. Jose kept his attention divided between Chloe and Netty, and Wil's dissemination of information regarding their new living quarters.

Quietly, Cobby followed Abby. As he entered the alcove, he was ambushed by wings, strands of golden hair, and the captivating mouth of the Elder he loved. Stepping back, Abby grinned up at him. Ruefully, he searched over his back.

"We better be careful, love, unless you're ready to announce our relationship to everyone."

29

Her grin drooped. "*No*, not yet, Cobby. Everything is so new and scary. I still need to think about what this means."

Cobby cupped her face in his hands, brushing her lips with his. "It means we love each other. That's what people do. They fall in love."

Abby cast her face down. "But you know I have other considerations, Cob. I need to figure out what to do about Jose first. I don't want him hurt. And what about the Womb? It might have something in store for me that prevents us from being together."

Cobby's eyes lit up as he caressed her abdomen. "This is our baby in here if Echo is to be believed. I'm not going to let anything prevent me from being a full-time father to our baby. I didn't get the chance with Kane." He grinned. "This is Kane's half-brother. And you're going to need me." The smile appeared back on Abby's lips, hope and anticipation mixing with her love for Cobby. They embraced tightly, completely missing the movement at the entranceway that disappeared as quickly as it appeared.

"Abby," begged Cobby, "just give me some more time. I'll work something out. I need to make sure Bonnie and Chloe are stable then I'll speak to Netty. I'll tell her everything."

Abby closed her fingers over Cobby's protesting lips, adding hers to the bargain. "Shh . . . we can trust her. The female Elders have the power. As much as she's nuts about Wil, the male Elders aren't as important as the females." Abby's eyes gleamed with wild luminosity. "That might make all the difference, Cobby." She glanced down, placing her hand over his. "Now that there's another life involved . . . our baby . . . everything has changed. I want the baby to have two loving parents that are together."

Cobby embraced her again. "What will you tell Jose?"

"I don't know yet. But I hope he would want me happy." Abby sighed. "I just plain don't think he'll take it well."

"Shhh, my love. Let's take it slow. We have so much to deal with right now. Just know I'm here and waiting." Cobby released her with a soft kiss. "Now go. You first. We'll talk again when we can." Squeezing her hand, Cobby turned her toward the exit whispering, "I love you."

As the couple weaved their separate ways back to the group,

rooms were being assigned for sleeping. Netty held court, explaining, "Perhaps it would be better if the women requested supplies. The men can deliver furniture to the respective rooms." She turned to Bonnie and Chloe. "I think it would be best if you didn't sleep alone for a while." She then nodded to Abby. "Why don't the three of you bunk together?"

Abby spoke up brightly. "Of course, Netty. I understand completely."

"I don't think that's a good idea, Abby," Jose spoke up darkly.

Abby tried to soothe Jose. "It's just until they're better. Chloe is almost in her last month and will deliver sometime in the near future. She needs help."

Chloe spoke up. "We'll send her back to you eventually, Jose. I can really use the help now." She turned to Bonnie who sat on the ground, oblivious to all, with Dezi and Hud supporting her. "And you know we can't leave Bonnie alone. So it's settled. Maybe you could go order us the beds, Netty? Something bright and cheerful."

"I'll start on the men's beds. That okay with you guys?" Dezi and Hud nodded affirmatively at Cobby who then turned back into the alcove. Abby soon followed, leaving storm clouds from Jose in her wake.

Wil conferred with Netty then signaled for Baby and Echo to follow him.

"No . . . I need Echo here," cried Chloe. "Don't leave me, Echo."

Soothing tentacles reached out to her mind.

"I will never leave you, Sister Chloe. We are bonded. I must be here to help with Brother Scotty's offspring. It is my sworn duty to protect those that loved my Brother. You are my family. I give you my promise. I will not be long. This is my chance to meet my Oolahan family formally for the first time. They are waiting for Brother Wil to deliver me."

Chloe waddled over to Echo and Wil. She held out her arms and Echo flew into them to receive his hug. "Hurry back, Echo. I don't think I can sleep without you near."

"I promise to return, my Sister. Do not fret."

With a flutter of wings, Echo left, Wil trailing behind.

"We will be back in the morning," Netty said. "Dezi, I will work with you to set up your kitchen and explain how to retrieve supplies. For now, you will find water and something to eat waiting for you on a table in the next room that will serve as your kitchen."

She glanced down at their doggie entourage: Barney, Teddy, Penny, King and Queenie, the royal pit-bull, all so quiet and listless. "We will need to bring them to the labs tomorrow. They must be checked out. There is no telling what the effects of the portal may have done to them."

Chloe cried out in dismay, encouraging Teddy to come to her side where she held him tightly to her chest.

"I must go join Wil and Echo. Come, Baby." Taking Baby's hand, they watched as he scurried up into Netty's arms, leaving the new survivors to settle down and contemplate the extraordinary luck visited upon them again as the last survivors of Earth and the long-term impact on their mental health.

# Chapter 5

Netty hustled Baby down the vast inner corridor of soaring space to join the horde of minions gathered to celebrate Echo's arrival on Oolaha. Trailing behind them, flocks of nooglets and minions hovered, anxious to join the celebration.

As Netty neared her destination, she heard a most recognizable shriek. *"Mama."* Seventy pounds of feathers, swishing tail and little-girl Elder exploded as Maya threw herself at her mother.

"Can I go to the party, Mama? Please? I want to go to Echo's party.*"*

Netty disentangled herself from Maya's grip around her legs and picked up her daughter. "No sweetie, you need to stay with the babies." She held Maya's face in one hand, turning it to and fro for an inspection.

"How do you feel, baby girl?"

"I feel fine, Mama. How do *you* feel?" she asked, throwing her skinny arms amok.

Netty laughed at her antics. She glanced at Baby, quietly waiting.

"Do you think . . . ?" Netty cocked an eyebrow at Baby as she set Maya down.

"Sister Maya is very welcome at the celebration. She is a second-generation Elder and treasured." Baby slipped his hand inside Maya's tiny fingers and off they went, Maya dancing and laughing in her excitement.

Within thirty minutes, the threesome stood before the vast coliseum that held Baby's thousands of brother and sister minions. They sat in layers against the Womb walls, some attached as if "feeding", some simply seated on the shelves that lined the enormous room from top to bottom. Netty hushed Maya as the absence of sound waves created a reverent atmosphere; almost like a church. From the multitude of minions came a significant mind stroke. It was Echo.

"Come down to the dais, Sister Netty. We are waiting for you."

Baby, Netty and Maya followed a minion-lined path that opened for them. Thousands and thousands of glowing eyes followed them as they maneuvered their way to the middle of the gently sloping floor to claim the chairs waiting for them. Wil sat alongside Echo, comfortable and expectant.

"Your wings are beautiful, Sister." A strange minion appeared before her.

Echo's luminous trills saturated her mind.

"This is Brother Forbation. He is our oldest existing minion." With a flourish of his golden leather arms, Echo presented his Brother and stepped back.

Forbation appeared slight and bent, his mind auras swirling yet peaceful. Netty felt a profound sense of wellbeing and wisdom.

"We have much to thank you for, Sister Netty. Tonight is a celebration we have long awaited." Forbation's hands came together then reached out to Netty. She gave him her hand. "You have returned Baby and Echo to our family."

"Without Baby, we would have never recovered the use of our wings. It is his discovery of the chemical interaction between minions and Elders that restored our long-dead ability. Our history says it was part of our punishment from the Womb for making man in our own image." The old minion bent at the waist then turned to face the coliseum. As he slowly raised both his arms wide, thousands and thousands of golden minions took to the air, glowing and sparkling, dancing on air.

Netty and Wil held their heads with the impact of thousands of auras assailing them at once.

Netty's eyes scanned the vastness of the coliseum, catching sight of wisps of fire trailing the odd minion or two. Forbation slowly lowered his arms. Instantly, the minions fluttered to the sides of the Womb walls and settled into their perches.

The wise old minion backed into his chair next to Echo. His seat was placed higher than the others in the line, as befitted a minion of his stature. An empty seat begged company by his other side. Patting it softly with his leather fingers, he motioned Baby to his side.

With a glance at Netty, Baby lumbered to the seat next to Forbation with Netty taking a seat in line next to Wil and Echo.

As she trained her sights on the minions around her, she saw them part to create a pathway. Walking down the pathway was the navigator minion with the fire butterfly attached to her antler. In her hands, she held a ruby-glass tray on which sat two fire butterflies that emanated a spicy lemon fragrance. Silence permeated the coliseum as Minion IV slowly approached Forbation and bowed. As Forbation raised his hand toward Baby and Echo, they rose to stand before him. Minion IV handed the tray to Forbation, who placed it on his chair after rising.

Minion IV placed her hands on Baby's face and silently conveyed her respect. She then turned to Echo, her hands on Echo's face as the exercise was repeated, then she melted into the crowd.

All eyes were on Forbation as he placed a butterfly on Baby's crystal antler, then on Echo's. The butterflies lit up in flaming glory, throwing sparks and trails of fire behind them as they firmly attached to their new homes, appendages sinking deeply into the minion's antlers to stop at the emulsion contained inside.

Forbation's aura resounded with delight as every living creature in the room absorbed his mind words.

"Brother Baby has brought great pride and acclaim to his lineage. He has uncovered the mystery that robbed us of our ability to fly for millions of years. Without his accidental creation of the new Elders we would be in the dark forever. For this deed, he deserves the highest honor a minion can win. One of the fabled fire butterflies from the vanquished plant, Aron." He turned his bent frame to Echo.

"Sister Echo, our long-lost new family member, has brought great pride and acclaim to her lineage. Without her dedication to her humans and the wildlife the Womb entrusted to them, they would have been lost when the final intervention vanquished yet another doomed planet. We grant you this great honor with exquisite pleasure."

Raising his arms in tribute, the minions again took to the air. The golden flight of the celebrants lit up the room, ablaze in color and the occasional glimpse of a minion with its own fire butterfly won from one dangerous campaign or another.

Baby and Echo stood holding hands and staring in wonderment, overcome with the emotion of being home at last, and feted by one and all. Occasionally they would turn to Wil and Netty for reassurance, proud to see them relaxed and smiling.

A sudden commotion parted the crowd once more as a time-worn but determined white, curly-haired, wingless but loyal Barney made his way to Echo's side and curled at her feet. Echo slipped her free hand down to pat his head, sending an aura of triumph to Netty and Wil.

"My Barney is with me."

Netty and Wil sent their proud feelings to Echo. Together they watched the display until the minions began to settle down again. The enormous room descended into solemn thoughts as Forbation nodded to Baby and Echo, sending them back to their seats, Barney trailing closely behind them both.

Forbation removed the rose-glass tray from his seat and held it aloft. The crowd of minions moved back and the floor in front of the dais slid back, revealing a gaping maw. As everyone watched, a translucent throbbing mass emerged from the depths, the smell of organic mustiness stronger. It stopped as it rose a few inches from the floor, its bulk still resting under their feet, its mystery hidden by the floor.

Netty gripped her chair at the unaccustomed hammering of her heart. Glancing at Wil, she could feel his emotions racing in tune with hers.

"We accept the need to terminate life as directed by the Womb. Yet our hearts bleed with the necessity. This is a tribute to the wisdom of the Womb and our own private anguish for the elimination of life, necessary though it may be." Forbation's aura dimmed. The ruby glass tray in his upraised hand exploded, sprinkling ruby dust down on the gelatinous throbbing mass that had risen from the depths of the floor where it melted quickly into the frightening creature.

A sudden flutter above her head made Netty look up. The minions had gathered in line and one by one; they flew over the mass, dipping down to place a hand on the throbbing mystery. Netty watched as one of their antlers split to spill out a red droplet that fell to be absorbed just as the ruby tray had been.

Wil and Netty swapped puzzled glances.

Forbation stood watching the procession. It was clear the ritual would consume hours. At a nod, Baby and Echo approached. Their antlers opened and red drops emerged, the antlers closing behind. They each took their red drop in leather hands and lobbed them into the maw to be absorbed.

They turned to face Wil and Netty.

"We must return to the others now. It is time to sleep." With those words, Baby, Echo, Barney, Wil and Netty bowed and waved to Forbation, getting a slow nod in return.

"We will talk again, Sister and Brother," Forbation said.

The small group made their way back to the survivors' quarters after returning Maya to the children's section. They were full of wonderment at what they had witnessed. Baby and Echo were oddly silent, avoiding all mind queries.

The minions of Oolaha continued to pay their respects to the Womb, well into the night.


Wil and Netty entered the survivors' quarters along with Baby, Echo and Barney, who hurried off to find Chloe. A few tired and restless survivors waited for them, peppering them with questions.

"I'm very happy for Baby and Echo. I'm sure it means a lot to be back with their own kind . . . their family," said Hud, his voice trailing off with a broken sob.

Abby hurried to his side, her arm snaking around his shoulders. He held his head in his hands, rubbing his face, shoulders quivering silently. Looking up, they watched the quiet tears course down his face.

"I have yet to hear what we're going to do to look for my wife. And Peter. You saw how Bonnie is. I don't know if she'll survive this if we don't find him. There's been too much loss. Her mother . . . Johno and Crystal . . . the others . . ." His voice broke. "Ginger Mae was her best friend." He stared into the face of his fellow survivors, emotions razor-thin. "How am I to go on without Ginger Mae? She's everything . . ." Shaking his head, he swallowed, unable to speak.

"Try not to make yourself sick over this, Hud. We need information before we can come up with a plan. Netty . . . do you know what our first step should be?" Abby appealed to her mentor.

"I don't know, my dear. Let's see if Baby or Echo can answer some questions." The words were still resonating around the room when the two minions proudly entered, Chloe on their heels. Their new butterflies sat preening on their antlers, dancing light from their trails of fire that reflected on the walls of the Womb.

Chloe settled into a comfortable round chair with huge red and green spots; an obvious attempt at someone's idea of pleasing décor. "I can't sleep," she said, rubbing her huge abdomen, her bright eyes radiating admiration for the sparks of fire highlighting the minion's fire butterflies.

Netty turned to Baby who was settling in Wil's lap.

"I know what you seek, Sister. I am not the one with the answers. We must speak with a navigator. If anyone can give hope to Sister Bonnie and Brother Hud it would be one of them. Unfortunately, they are all spoken for. Their talent is valuable and much in need. Perhaps a meeting with Brother Forbation will be of great value."

Netty nodded her head as her brain absorbed the auras that saturated her mind. "Baby, I have a question if you don't mind. I understand the solemnness of the celebration we attended tonight but may I inquire into the meaning of the offerings everyone made to the . . . eh . . . entity in the floor?"

Hud and the rest of the survivors listened closely as Wil and Netty related the mystery of the ceremony they had witnessed.

Many of the survivors cringed upon hearing of the recipient of the offering. "I don't understand, girl. What the heck was that all about?" demanded Jose.

Baby and Echo moved towards each other, joining hands. They bowed their heads together as they sent mind auras to everyone. The tentative nature of the auras confused the survivors. Finally, the minions sat on the floor and began.

"The Womb is a singular life force, unlike anything in existence anywhere. We don't know when the Womb came into being nor do we always understand the reasons behind its directives. A few principles are very clear. The Womb is our creator. We are eternally grateful for the life that has been granted to us. It is our aim to live up to the honor even as we are reminded of our ancestors' transgressions and fall from grace. Yes, we have been punished but luckily, the Womb is sometimes forgiving. It is part of our culture that whenever a species or an intervention brings about the eradication of life, we honor the Womb's decision with a sacrifice of our own. It is in recognition of the other life lost and the sparing of our lives when we disobeyed the Womb; creating life from our own cells that would evolve into you, my Brother and Sisters."

Baby continued. "What you saw at the ceremony was the giving of a part of ourselves to the Womb in respect. Our antlers hold the precious emulsion that contains our defense system. Without that we would perish when we visit other civilizations for study. It is our only protection and our most valued possession. A befitting sacrifice under the circumstances, don't you agree?"

Baby glanced around at the blank faces of the humans. Cobby was the first to speak.

"I'm sure we will understand in time, Baby. But if the Womb felt humans no longer deserved to live, yet allowed us to live, why destroy the entire planet?"

This time it was Echo who answered. "I am so sorry, Brother Cobby. But it was not the decision of the Womb to let you live. The planet didn't stand a chance once the Womb realized the evil in man would never change. It will always be there. The propensity for violence, the coveting of that which does not belong to humans . . . It was Brother Forbation that saved you. In his wisdom, he saw a reason to warn us by sending the nooglets to us. If we could complete our task of turning the wildlife back to the Hive and into the portal we would be allowed to save other life. The life we have come to love. You . . . my Brothers and Sisters."

"But what about all the others, Echo? You loved them too." Cobby kneaded his knotted brow, grief for his friends dripping from his voice. The aura came slow . . . soft . . . contrite.

"Time, Brother. Time. So much happened . . . unplanned for. Time just ran out."

A sob was heard from Abby, her tail flexing madly in the air. "But why the entire planet Echo . . . *why?*"

Baby raised his glowing eyes to look them all in the face. His aura weighed heavily in their minds, dim and slow.

"Earth was doomed anyway, my Brothers and Sisters. The Womb only exacerbated the process. The meteor that was headed toward Earth would have done everlasting damage. It was stuck in a gravitational tug of war with a larger planet. It would have altered the tilt of the Earth, sending it into a new orbit with the sun. The new orbit would have taken it far from the life-giving rays of the sun that creates the temperate climate needed to sustain life. As the Earth's new orbit took it further away, it would not return close enough to melt the frozen crust of the planet for eleven years. And that would only occur after the numerous volcanoes of the planet blanketed the atmosphere with ash. Everything left after the initial collision would die, slowly." Baby's aura paused.

"Normally a planet called Saturn would have protected Earth from the deadly meteor. Saturn is huge compared to Earth but its size diminishes a fraction every year, allowing space debris to slip by and lessening the power of the ricochet of debris into deep space, thereby protecting Earth. It was only a matter of time. The nudge given by the Womb was actually more humane."

Maniacal laughter was heard from the entrance to a new bedroom. It was Bonnie.

"You all sit here whining about the past. That's rich. We are all alive. We're the lucky ones. We can't do anything about those that were left behind. They're gone. *Gone, you hear?*" She pounded her fist on the palm of her hand, her tear-streaked face red and swollen. Her eyes blazed with pain and insanity. "Where is my husband? Where?" Her fists slapped her palm in rhythm with her bitter words. Her eyes flashed madly, searching. "Hud? *Tell them.* We need to find Ginger Mae." She ran to Hud, her fists on his chest, her face upraised beseechingly. "Pretty please, Hud? Make them understand. Make them find Peter. *I need to find Peter.*" Her voice rose hysterically.

Kenya turned her face into Kane's chest and began to cry softly. Reflections of anguish remained on everyone's faces as Hud slipped his arms under Bonnie's legs and, with a nod to Netty, carried Bonnie back to the bedroom, Netty trailing behind.

The room filled with silence, Kenya's sobs finally trailing off. Jose stood slowly, a mystified expression overtaking his sadness. "Does anyone hear that?"

Cobby spoke up. "Hear *what?*" They all listened intently. "I don't hear anything."

"Well, *I* certainly do." Jose hurried into the hallway that led to the blocked pathway, marking the entrance to the rest of the Womb. He stopped suddenly as he witnessed overhead the hurried flight of hundreds of minions heading outside where the clang of a signal called them. The rest of the survivors hurried after him.

Abby called to Echo. "Hurry, girl. Something's going on." The hallway lit up as Echo and Baby entered with their fire butterflies firmly attached. Baby fluttered into the air, joining the flow of minions. Within minutes, he was back on the ground with the survivors.

"We must go back. There is great danger."

Jose waved Baby away, flipping caution to the wind. "What possible danger could we be in? We're here on Oolaha. Nothing bad happens here. This is where the Womb lives, for heaven's sake." He dashed outside with the minions, the survivors trailing reluctantly.

A scene of haphazard chaos met their eyes. Minions were dropping from the sky like leaden raindrops, shrinking back out of the way as Forbation stood hunched over, swatting at them with a glistening ebony stick. From across the field a sphere was being gravitated their way, a few minions fluttering above. The strange moon of their new planet shed green-tinged light on the haphazard scene, throwing long sinister shadows over the landscape. As the sphere drew closer, the multitude of minions heeded Forbation's admonitions and wobbled their way far from the path. Baby threw out his golden arms, reflexively protecting his survivor family.

"What the heck is going on?" Jose demanded. He stepped out toward the path to the sphere, Echo's aura pleading with him for great caution. Everyone froze as the sphere approached, seemingly of its own volition.

The closer it got, the more it became clear something was wrong. The sphere was rolling, not gliding as it should have been. The minions that controlled the gravitational device fluttered helplessly high in the sky. Jose could make out a form inside the sphere, vague and sinuous.

Suddenly, as the sphere stopped in front of Jose, a golden bullet with a fire butterfly on her antler shot from inside the Womb. She was carrying a large sack. Flying above the sphere, Navigator IV dumped the contents of the sack on the sphere. They watched as it flowed down the sides where they could plainly see a network of spider fractures spreading across the surface of the sphere. But not before Jose glimpsed the most amazing sight.

Inside the sphere stood what appeared to be an eight-foot-tall sunflower, its form curvy and slender as if to model the human female form. Its olive leaves branched out like arms, gripping the sphere from side to side. But it was its flower that most entranced Jose. It sparkled with the power of the sun, gleaming, glowing and hot.

Inside the almost molten head of the flower peered eyes, sensuous and becoming; they were looking straight at Jose. *What the heck . . . is that thing flirting with me?*

"Brother Jose, please look away from the trypid. It is very dangerous. It does not belong here. Please, please . . . I must *insist.*" Forbation raised his ebony stick at Jose. Luckily he managed to get another glimpse of the enchanting creature before the substance from IV's bag sealed the fragmenting sphere for good. And what a glimpse it was. For in the very last seconds, he could swear that it bared a human-like breast with its leafy appendage and fluttered long lashes over the beguiling eyes and sculptured cheekbones of his beloved Abby.

Jose swiveled his head madly. "Did you see that, Kane? Kenya?" He peered over their shoulder spying the elusive Daisy hanging back in the shadows cast by the moon. "*Abby.* Where's Abby?"

"Hey, Daisy. Come on over here."

She approached slowly.

"Come on, kid. What're you doing hanging back there like a wallflower? You're supposed to be a star now. Do you mind telling me what was up with that creature?"

Before Daisy could speak, the sphere was attacked by the minions. Dozens more flew to the sphere to empty their sacks of the contents, encapsulating the creature inside.

Jose felt a sudden tug on his chest. He looked down, seeing nothing. The tug came again as he watched the IV minion navigate the sphere into the Womb to disappear. The strange tugs stopped. The flying minions landed on the ground to huddle with Forbation, the ancient minion, wildly gesticulating and throwing black auras into the minds of the bystanders. As the crowd of minions took back up into the sky to flit directly into the Womb, Forbation turned to the survivors and headed their way.

He cast his aura into their minds, the darkness and thunderous aura instilling alarm and fear. Failing to understand, they grouped tightly together, fully reminded that Oolaha was a new world and they were at its mercy.

Jose began to whimper. He screwed up his courage to speak as everyone else cowered with trepidation, not knowing what might happen next. "Where's Abby? *I saw her.* That thing has *Abby.*"

Forbation's aura lightened, trying hard to exert calm. "No, my Brother. The thing that you saw was a trypid. It is an evil and monstrous creature." Forbation wiped his hand across his brow. He looked to the sky in supplication. "Womb, forgive us."

"What is going on here, Forbation?" Netty strolled up to the group, her lion-like tail held high, Abby and Cobby trailing her.

Jose gasped in surprise. "Where have you been, Abby?"

Netty raised her hand for silence. "We passed minions in the hallway. They are frantic. I feel deep disturbance."

Forbation nodded. "It is cause for concern, Sister. But fear not. We will contain the menace. It has just caught us by surprise. We prayed we had seen the last of this species."

Jose looked up in doubt. "Menace? It looked harmless to me. What are you doing to the poor thing, Forbation?"

"It is none of your concern, Brother Jose. Please take the rest of the survivors back inside. I ask that you stay in your quarters and get some sleep." Forbation turned to leave.

"You will learn of the dangers of other life forms soon enough. They are not all benevolent like my species. Good night."

With those cryptic words, Forbation hobbled back to the Womb, disappearing from sight. The survivors were left with nothing to do but follow his advice.

# Three Days AE (After Earth)

# Chapter 6

Ginger Mae wondered how long she'd been held captive. All she knew was overwhelming loneliness and pain. No longer did sleep promise her a temporary sanctuary. From time to time she would reach out after being awakened by the hot burning smell that propelled her from her nightmares. The pervasive odor of terror that accompanied her captors penetrated her senses with strains of fear just as Pavlov's dogs salivated over their own stimulus. Only Ginger Mae's stimulus was that of dread that fortunately receded as she awoke, leaving her to discover a fresh batch of protein mush and chalky water. Wonderful, cool, healing water.

She pulled herself upright and allowed the fingers on her healthy arm to be her eyes that searched greedily for the source of the water. She fumbled along the floor until they hit upon the container. She carefully lifted it to her lips that had lost their tight parched feeling. No longer did her throat burn and feel scorched when she swallowed her saliva or the sustenance her captors left for her. She was healing.

Well . . . at least her body was. Her mind still functioned in a panic, her dreams confusing and scary. She propped herself into a sitting position as she ate, trying to dismiss the puzzle that the residue of anxiety from her dreams left behind. All she could remember was the faceless, nebulous bodies that surrounded her in her dreams. They seemed to pull at her as their arms tried to reach for her, yet never made contact; with the exception of one hand. One large hand that she swore she could actually feel. She rubbed her shoulder where the heavy hand had touched, her skin alive and strangely tingling. She felt an unexplained yearning to feel the touch again.

Dismissing the dream as just a manifestation of her loneliness, she lay back down and absently picked at the bandages across her eyes.

Her body froze as a sound reached her ears. She held her breath, her heart tripping faster than she could use the oxygen it pumped to her brain. Forcing herself to calm down, she slowed her breath to listen; the darkness suddenly alive with possibilities.

She froze again. Was that a scrape? The sound disappeared as she strained her ears to catch the direction from which it came, but all they registered was silence.

Ginger Mae lay like a rock but her senses were on fire. Desperation finally made her sit up again as her enclosure engulfed her with its silence. Tentatively, she spoke, keeping her voice low and tremulous.

"*Hello?* Is anyone there? I won't hurt you. Please . . . can you speak to me?" Her only response was silence. Not one to give up, she tried to rise to her feet in an unsteady manner, falling back on her mat in frustration. Her injured wrist began to throb again, waking up hundreds of nerve endings that sent messages of hot, livid agony to her confused brain.

Gritting her teeth and taking long controlled breaths, she rose to her knees. Using her good arm to help propel her, she crawled away from her pallet. It was time to explore her prison. Maybe then she could assess her possibility of escape more intelligently. If she actually discovered the source of the sounds . . . well she would wait and see. But as much as she was loath to admit it to herself, she knew the sounds had been a leftover manifestation of her dreams and the loneliness of the dark that threatened to consume her.

Working slowly and cautiously, she tried to keep her bearing as she moved in a straight line. Her knees quickly rebelled from the rough floor of her prison, clearly not built for comfort. When she could no longer tolerate the punishment to her knees, she stood up on her feet. Throwing out her arms, she attempted to stabilize herself, her head reeling with vertigo. *How can that be if I can't see?*

Her dizziness thankfully receding, she inched her feet forward; one tiny step at a time. She held her good arm out before her and kept her injured one close to her waist to protect it, the wrapping on it heavy and cumbersome.

Under her breath, she counted each tiny step until she reached the number sixty one. Unless she'd started from the opposite wall, she imagined her enclosure wasn't as small as she'd originally thought. She slid her good arm wide along the wall confronting her. It was a hard surface of a material she couldn't identify; cold to the touch with the feeling of pliant marble. *Pliant marble?* she asked herself as the wall gave under pressure from her hand.

Giving her body a quarter turn, she traced the now frigid wall with her hand as she continued counting her small steps, hoping to understand the complete contour of the room and wind up back at her pallet where she could take refuge against the increasing cold.

She made her way along the wall with her wrap held tightly for warmth. She counted under her breath. *Forty five, forty six, forty seven . . . Ow!* Down she went with a resounding thud, her hand hitting flesh that moved with a groan to push her off onto the floor.

Realizing she'd just tripped over something alive, her nerves battled with her fight or flight response. Her loneliness won. Swallowing, she moistened her lips and breathed deeply, her voice seemingly absent.

"Hello?" she whispered. The silence threatened to overwhelm her. She reached out to touch, encountering a human shoulder. She shrank back, surprised. She admitted to herself that she'd fully expected an injured creature.

"Hello, can you hear me?" She ran her hand across his muscular chest, fumbling on his face. Her fingers danced lightly, absorbing his features. She felt the stubble of his beard confirming his sex and allowing her to guess he was mature. Her heart sang with the possibility he could help her.

The man groaned again and smacked his lips, his hand reaching up to clutch at her wrist—luckily her good one—and pulling her down to his face.

"Wa . . . ter, pl . . . pls." The man mumbled and choked but she knew what he needed. Wrenching her arm away, she stood to inch her way back, retracing her steps and carefully counting her way. She couldn't afford to get lost now.

Finding her way slowly back to her pallet, she knelt to feel for her protein mush and water. She could hear louder whines from the man as he reacted to her absence.

"Hold on, please. I'm getting you water." She made her way back to the wall, carefully counting her steps, her burden held awkwardly, pressed between her good arm and her body.

She set the food and water on the floor when her foot signaled she had returned to the man. Ineptly, she tried to cradle water to his mouth after locating his nose.

"Easy . . . easy." As the man insatiably lapped the water, it spilled all over her lap, further chilling her. Guttural sounds fermented deep in his throat, scaring her. She set the food and water down and carefully moved away, back to the security of the wall. She listened as the man continued to consume her supplies. The noise finally stopped with a sigh.

He cleared his throat, his voice low and dejected. "I . . . I'm sorry . . . please don't judge me by this. I've been through hell. I'm just . . . just not myself."

She sat silently weighing a response. She thought she heard a sob, melting some of her caution. She desperately needed an ally. Inching forward, she moved back to the man.

"Who are you?" she asked eagerly. "Where are you from? Have you been here long? Can you tell me your name?" Her questions were met with silence. A minute ticked by and Ginger Mae began to doubt her chances of finding help from this man. She gave him a nudge with her foot, hitting what appeared to be his bandaged wrapped arm and getting a sudden scream for her efforts.

She quickly sat down. "I'm so sorry. I didn't mean to hurt you. I can't see." The screaming subsided to a low moaning.

"They took my hand. They took it . . ."

She recoiled in horror. "They *took* your hand?" The thought left her speechless. His groaning turned to a whimpering as he spilled out some of his story.

"I don't know where I am or how I got here." Sobbing between his sentences, he made it clear how useless he would be. "I can't see either. I've had this bandage on my eyes as long as I can remember. They . . . they came for my hand a day or so ago."

She remembered the strange sounds she'd heard as if in a dream. "I'm so confused. I thought I was alone here. Do you remember when I was brought in?"

Her hands began to roam carefully over his face. She felt the bandages on his eyes. "I have the same bandages. I seem to recall I had problems seeing when they brought me here. Then I had . . . I think . . . a dream or something and when I woke up, I had these." She felt her loosening bandages.

"I don't know when you came in. I was in pretty bad shape. Vomiting . . . so sick." His voice was getting stronger.

"Yeah . . . me too. And the smell made me sicker. Did you smell it, too? Like something bad was burning?"

"Yeah. I get a creepy feeling of dread when I smell it. It usually means they're going to take me. It's never a good thing."

She sat in the dark and examined his voice with her ears. His tones were friendly but confused. His crying had stopped and he seemed more rational now. She needed more information. Much more.

"You haven't answered me. Where are you from? Who are you?" These seemed to be the wrong questions to ask as he clammed up again. "Can't you answer me? What's the big deal? I'm not going to do anything to you, for Pete's sake. I can hardly walk as it is."

He finally broke his silence. "It's not that. I just . . . just . . . don't *know*."

"Just don't know *what*?"

"I don't know who I am or what I'm doing here, where I'm from. I can't remember *anything.*"

"Are you kidding me? How can that be?" *Oh . . . my . . . God.* She stopped cold, goose bumps crawling up her back. She reacted as if hit by a steam shovel. Overtaken by a bottomless fright she realized she didn't know her own name, or where she was from either. She'd been so preoccupied with what was happening to her she hadn't even realized. She remembered thinking she needed to get back to . . . to where? Her insides began to crawl, snakes making tracks inside her where her confidence used to be. *Who am I? I know I'm me but . . . who am I?*

"You okay?" the man asked. She shook her head, trying to clear the feelings of abandonment that overtook her.

"No," she whispered. "I am very much *not* okay." She tried to blink her eyes inside their bandages, wetness testifying to her unconscious tears. She reached out her good arm to find the stranger's remaining hand. She felt a reassuring squeeze from him.

His tone was low, almost a whisper matching hers. "Go ahead say it. You don't remember either."

Ginger Mae choked with emotions. "How did you know?"

"Just goes to reason. We seem to be in the same predicament. You're just a bit luckier than me."

"Why do you say that?" She wrinkled her nose in puzzlement.

"Well, dear lady. You have both of your hands and probably all of your hair."

Ginger Mae snorted. "If you can call that *lucky*." She leaned in toward his voice. "Do you mind?" Without waiting for an answer, she held out her hand to locate his head. She slowly ran her questing fingers over his bald pate, free of shaving stubble, warm and smooth. "You used to have hair. Before you came here . . . ?"

He reached up with his remaining hand to cover hers. He brought their hands down to rest at his side. "Sorry, I guess I'm just not used to it yet."

"I noticed your head is smooth. Shouldn't you have stubble if they shaved your hair off?" She had completely misunderstood. "It's a lot easier to get used to something like that than the blindness caused by these infernal bandages."

The man released a sigh. "I guess you're right. It's just one more hard adjustment at a time where I seem to have no control over anything. That's not easy for a man who has been so darn independent his whole life."

"How do you *know* you've been independent? You can't remember anything." She hoped he was wrong and their memory would come back. She *had* to bank on that or she would just lose it right here, right now.

"It's just a feeling I have. That's all. As a matter of fact, I think we should get rid of these damned bandages. I can't go another

50

second not seeing. And if we're going to figure out how to get out of here, we need to be able to *see*, damn it."

Ginger Mae felt the man remove his hand that covered hers. She sensed him working at his bandages.

"They feel like they're ready to come off, anyway." She heard the sound of adhesive parting, and the man laughed with a sense of relief.

"It's okay . . . I can *see*. The light hurts." A moment of silence.

"Okay, it's your turn. I think you need to take yours off, too. Let's see if you can see anything."

Ginger Mae raised her hands to her eyes, her bandages already loose. She felt for a slack end she could unravel as she wondered at the new note in the man's voice. Scratching insistently at a pucker in the bandages, she slowly unwound them and tossed them aside.

Her eyes remained closed, her trepidation getting the best of her. The man found her hand and gave it a squeeze, his voice strange with apprehension. "It's okay. You can get through this."

Ginger Mae slowly opened her eyes. The gummy residue of accumulated inactivity failed to obliterate the fact that she could, indeed, see. The light caused her to blink and squint painfully but she felt her eyes would be alright.

"You have beautiful blue eyes." His statement drew her attention.

She examined the man in front of her. He had a wide, trusting face and fair complexion although muddy and slack. His frame looked muscular and healthy under the circumstances. At the moment, his face had arrayed itself in a demeanor of compassion, of all things.

"What's the matter? Not what you expected? And for your information, my eyes are brown."

The man laughed, his face lit up by his effervescent smile. The sound was wonderful to her ears. So human . . .

"My dear, you have the most amazing crystal blue eyes. No one would make a mistake about that." He laughed again.

"Honestly. I know what color my eyes are. And they're brown. " The man stopped laughing, his face sobering again with a look of pity. He reached out to her shoulder as if to pick off a piece of lint.

He held out his hand for her to see.

There, resting in his palm was a thick strand of blond hair. He dropped it in her lap and plucked another strand off her shoulder.

In a panic, she reached up to find her hair missing, minor clumps still adhering to her scalp. She trailed her quavering fingers through them, her face crumbling as they fell out into her hand. Her face dissolved into quiet tears, her shuddering frame announcing the final degrading humiliation as she stroked the useless strand of her female identity and femininity.

She looked up as the man, with a bashful look, knelt down and hesitantly took her into his good arm.

"I know it's harder for a woman. I'm sure it's quite a shock. But we're both still *alive.* Hold on to that. I think we have bigger problems, right now. We can *help* each other. I know I'm sure grateful as all hell to find I'm no longer alone."

Her sobbing abated in his embrace. He was right. At least she wasn't alone anymore. The terrors had receded a bit. She pulled away from him to look into his face. She studied the honest planes of his bones and realized what an attractive man he was, maybe a few years younger than her.

"I know you're right. It was . . . just a shock." She rubbed her traces of tears away and tried to smile. "Bad timing, I guess."

She glanced across the room to her pallet. She could see traces of her blond glossy hair littering the floor and her bed. She glanced back at the man's pallet. It was a mess with strewn covers, dried gruel from old portions of the protein slop they gave them to eat and water spilt everywhere from his water container that lay on its side.

"Well . . . I guess we can't cry over spilt milk, as they say. That goes for hair and water too." She gave a big sigh then turned back to her new companion, straightening her shoulders. "I'll be okay, thanks." She gave him a tiny smile.

He smiled back. "Atta girl." Together they rose to their feet, he wobbly, and she steadier.

"Why don't we move our stuff together?" she suggested. "We need to clean this place up. Then we need to take stock and try to make some kind of a plan. Agreed?" The man nodded his agreement and, with her help, gathered everything salvageable to carry over to her part of the room where they arranged their pallets side-by-side. A defense of two. Bald and broken but a defense none the less.

An hour later, they had cleaned up her area and arranged their pallets to their liking. They both quietly wondered what their hosts would make of the new arrangement and whether it might have any deleterious effect for them.

"Hey you . . . I'm beat with just that little work." Ginger Mae sat on her pallet and watched the man shove his broken water bottle in the corner with the rest of their small pile of detritus. He turned and gave her his now characteristic quiet grin. She watched it transform his face, lighting up his eyes.

"How long are we going to go on calling each other, *Hey you?*" he asked, his smile widening.

She reddened, her eyes becoming slits as she looked down at her legs. "Sorry. I guess we need to fix that somehow."

He watched her, amusement now dancing gaily on his face. "Well, why don't I name you and you can name me? I think that would work just fine," he suggested.

Getting into the spirit, newly bald Ginger Mae clapped her hands. "Okay. What should we name me?"

The man cocked his head and thought. "I have a name that just popped into my head. It's a pretty name, I think you'll like it. It's a happy name."

She shrugged her shoulders. "Let me have it," she said with reservation.

"How about, Bonnie?"

Ginger Mae tapped her finger against her chin in thought. "I like it. It's comfortable. And a happy name. Bonnie it is."

"And how about me?" The man looked hopeful.

Ginger Mae studied him, trying not to smile, showing him her serious intent.

"Since you are soon to become my lifesaver and figure out how to get us out of here, it needs to be something fitting. Something serious and strong." She looked deeply into his eyes and a fleeting thought popped into her head. "*Peter*. You look like a *Peter*."

He smiled with relief. "Peter it is, then." He walked carefully over to her and knelt down, extending his only hand.

"How do you do, Bonnie? My name is Peter."

She paused; a look of confusion crossed her face then quickly disappeared as she slid her hand into his.

"You have no idea how happy I am to meet you, Peter. I have a feeling we're going to be fast friends." They shook sincerely, hope now featured in both their newly seeing eyes.

# Four Days AE (After Earth)

# Chapter 7

Kenya paced madly, her exasperation with Bonnie pronounced in her footwork. *So much the better.* She knew she could hardly yell at the woman. Not when her own hubby was safe and sound tucking the baby in before tonight's memorial service.

She stopped her pacing and decided to try a new direction with Bonnie. Joining Chloe and Bonnie at the bed, she took one last look around the ridiculously decorated bedroom.

Polka dots and vibrant colors clashed with giant stuffed elephants. *Where in the world did Dezi get this stuff from? The Kreyven just happened to have them lying around?*

Rolling her eyes over the top of Bonnie's matted head, she signaled for Chloe to stand up, a task easier said than done as her pregnancy was just beginning its last month. Chloe groaned upon rising, her hands supporting her back.

"Come on, Bon. It just won't be the same without you," she said.

Kenya and Chloe both glanced at the purple plastic side table that contained bowls of food left untouched since lunchtime. Their eyes met as Kenya's hand gently stroked Bonnie's filthy hair.

"I know, chickey. It's hard losing your husband and your mother at the same time. I . . ."

Bonnie slammed her fist in her bedclothes.

"I didn't lose Peter. He's still alive. Now leave me alone. *Please.*" Bonnie turned her back to the room and her friends.

"Why don't you go ahead?" Kenya whispered to Chloe. With her eyebrows raised, Kenya nodded her head at her. "I'll meet you at the nursery. Tell Kane to wait for me." Reaching out, Kenya gave the other woman a quick hug. "Don't worry. I'm just going to try to talk some sense into her. This has been going on long enough."

Kenya watched Chloe plod out of the room, Bonnie's back unyielding. She quietly sidled onto the bed.

Her head whipped back to the door as a new sound drew her attention. She was surprised to see Hud and Abby standing there, the Elder's tawny tail twitching with tension as they tiptoed into the room.

"Are you coming?" Abby mouthed. Hud's expressively hopeful face and raised eyebrows revealed his feelings. Kenya gazed at the twosome sadly before she slowly shook her head, holding her finger to her lips to keep them silent. They bowed their heads, Abby slipping her arm around Hud. With a scooting motion of Kenya's hand, they crept back out of the room.

Taking a deep breath, Kenya let Bonnie have it.

"Well, you couldn't very well go anyway, smelling the way you do." Bonnie's shoulders stiffened. "Don't you think you're becoming a bit tiresome? We all have burdens to carry. We have *all* lost someone we loved: Scotty, Johno, Crystal, Ginger Mae and the others. You don't see Hud carrying on like this, do you?"

"Leave me alone, Kenya." The words dripped with venom; her shoulders remained frozen.

"It's been days now. How long are you going to stay cooped up in here not eating? Can you please take some time and think about the rest of us and get the heck off your pity pot? There's a lot of work that needs to be done and you need to do your share." Kenya held her breath, afraid she'd gone too far.

The unyielding shoulders moved. Bonnie turned her body back to face Kenya and sat up. Her face was blotchy and sallow, her hair hanging in clumps. She reached over to the nightstand and calmly raised a glass of water to her chalky lips. She set the glass down after a long drink and folded her arms back under the yellow and red striped bedcovers; more of Dezi's misguided efforts to cheer her up.

"I know what you're trying to do, Kenya, and it won't work. You can say what you want but I'm just not going." Her eyes filled with tears. "I know Peter is trying to find his way back to me. I need to be here when he arrives. He might not understand that we're even *here*. I think you can all do without me at the memorial service. I've made my peace with the loss of my mother. I was damned lucky to have her as long as I did. She was where she wanted to be. With Clyde. Now, *please* . . . don't even think about making me sit through a lot of sanctimonious garbage about my dead husband when he's *not* dead."

Kenya ran her hands through her chaotic curly auburn mop and kept her expression neutral as she rose. Striking back now would serve no one and destroy any headway she may have made.

"Well . . . if you change your mind . . ." she said stiffly and turned to leave.

"I won't," Bonnie called from her bed. "As a matter of fact, I'll be waiting at the portal. You were right about one thing. It's time I got out of bed and tried to get someone interested in helping me find Peter. If we're lucky, maybe Ginger Mae will turn up too."

Kenya stood at the door, trying to suppress her shock.

"You better wait until Netty gets back from the service. You can't just go wandering off by yourself. It's too dangerous."

Bonnie slipped from bed to yank on clothes that were already three days old and about as fresh as a tuna left in the noonday sun for twenty four hours. Her eyes glittered, feverish and mad.

"I'll be fine. I just need to find Tobi."

"Tobi? What in the world do you need Tobi for? You leave her alone. She has enough problems without you distracting her. We must have a least a dozen calves ready to be born." She put her hands to her hips in anger, all thought of Bonnie's tender sensibilities gone as her fear for Tobi's safety, so deeply ingrained over the decades, left her bristling.

Bonnie brushed past her looking like a demented slip of a ghost. Not a word was said as she focused on her destination and left Kenya behind.

The stunning new mom yanked on her hair in consternation. *I need Kane. Better yet . . . Baby or Echo.* She turned quickly on her heels and out of the survivors' quarters, her shapely caramel-cream legs flashing as she beat a hasty retreat to find Kane in the nursery.

\*\*\*

Bonnie sat in the grass with Tobi, both pensive and yet each feeling better for the support of her best friend. They had been through so much together over the decades. They sat in front of the opening of a sphere that Bonnie had identified as the one from where she'd emerged before the Earth exploded. On her lap lay the Bible she'd swiped from Dezi's room before leaving the survivors' quarters. She'd been surprised to see it there, wondering why it hadn't been taken for the use during the service.

*What difference does the damned book make, anyway? It's just full of lies told to cover the truth.* But in her heart, she knew the words could still give comfort and that's exactly what she needed now.

It hadn't been easy. First she'd had to find Tobi. Emerging from the Oolahan fortress, she had scanned the grassy horizon, seeing not a soul. The brightness of the alien sun beat down unmercifully, causing her to close her eyes in a tight squint, a headache writhing like a dervish in her heavy head. She swiped at the filthy hair that hung in her eyes. *Maybe I should have eaten something.* A dizzy spell caught her off balance.

In the distance, she could see the tops of the domes that housed the portals. She swallowed at what appeared to be hundreds of them. From time to time, she thought she saw a flashing blob of what could only be the Kreyven, rushing from portal to portal in its urgent business. Or what was more likely to be the Kreyven and its many duplicates doing the *Womb's* business.

She felt a wave of relief as her instinct took her to a grove of greenery represented by a giant curly-leaved tree that suspended its foliage like flexible pieces of giant, macaroni-shaped chlorophyll; so tempting to a hungry herd of elephants and their pregnant females. As she approached, she heard the expected familiar trumpet as Tobi separated herself from her herd to welcome her favorite human pal.

After the proper sloppy kisses, Tobi knelt down to assist Bonnie's climb up onto her broad back. From there, Bonnie could scan the horizon. She shaded her eyes, searching for other wildlife. Frowning in frustration, she glanced back at the gleaming minion fortress. The silence and inactivity were surprising. *Must be the memorial service.*

58

*At least I'll be left alone.* Urging Tobi forward, they headed toward the dome that contained the portal where she'd emerged the day Earth exploded. With Tobi's help, she dismounted, stumbling as she stepped onto the ground from Tobi's trunk.

*I'll show them,* she predicted. *I know what I'm talking about. How would I like it if the situation was reversed and Peter allowed himself to be deterred from* my *rescue?*

Her finger absently plucked at the sweet freshness of the well-clipped grass, tossing the shoots over to Tobi who snorted them greedily into her mouth with her trunk. She realized her heart was not really in it. As she looked around in a desultory way at the number of portal-covered spheres, she wondered again about Peter. She glanced inside the portal from Earth and got a thrill dreaming about how surprised Peter would be to find her waiting. Waiting . . . for how long? *I guess I'll wait forever. But that's no help to Peter.* Her spirits sagged and she rolled onto her side in a fetal position. Tobi's trunk roamed over her body. Low rumbles from deep in her belly vibrated through Bonnie's entire body.

"It's okay, girl. Don't worry about me."

"Why do you speak to this large animal?" From out of nowhere a tentative but sparkling finger stroked her mind. She sat up abruptly.

"Echo?" There was no response.

"Why do you not answer me, child?" The bright finger swirled in her brain.

Bonnie leaned her head back to find the sight of a golden minion fluttering its wings, its tail held straight up in the air, the thick, darker fur on the end twitching. Most notable was the stunning butterfly attached to the creature's antlers, trailing flame-like sparks as the butterfly's wings languidly caressed the air.

"I am not an *it*." Her mind felt the minion's indignation.

"Well, I am not a child." Bonnie's surliness embarrassed her. Offering the Oolahan a sign of contriteness, she patted the grass next to her.

"Please . . . come sit with us."

The minion gracefully descended from overhead, its own wings beating so rapidly they appeared invisible. Bonnie didn't get a good look until the creature landed and glided over the grass to select a spot a few inches from her.

The creature stared into Bonnie's eyes, twisting its head to the right, then to the left, its features scrunching up as it appeared to be searching for something. Bonnie inched backward on the grass facing the dome, the Bible slipping from her lap. Glimmering strokes caressed Bonnie's mind. The sensation relaxed her.

"You are one of the humans. Why are you not with the others in the great hall?"

Bonnie felt herself withdraw, the answer too private.

"You cannot hide from me, child. I can feel your depression and your anger. Are you not grateful you were saved from the fate of your planet and the rest of your humankind?"

Bonnie hung her head. "If it's any business of yours, I'm unhappy because my husband, Peter, is missing. I want to go find him but no one is listening to me." A tear leaked out from an eye and she wiped it away impatiently, looking up at the minion with a sudden hopeful surge. "Can *you* help me? Who are you exactly? Aren't you the one I saw a few days ago when we got here? You were aboard a sphere that came out of a portal."

"Yes," the creature answered. "I am an IV Navigator."

"IV? Ivey? You're a girl? And what is a navigator? You fly planes?"

"No, I don't fly planes, child. I comb the stars. I bounce from portal to portal in the service of the Womb. I locate planets or stars that the Womb has decreed in need of intervention. It might be because of the actions of a life form or just that the star is in jeopardy of causing damage to a planet as its magnetic pull increases or diminishes, throwing it into an altered orbit. Every action has a reaction that must be anticipated. I map the pathway, reporting back to the Womb who then decides the course of action and sends my Brothers or Sisters to begin the intervention."

"So you destroy life and planets like you did on Earth," Bonnie stated.

"You are misguided. We do no such thing. There are many levels of intervention. Sometimes the Womb decides to eliminate a destructive species to save many others. Sometimes it is a plant, sometimes a creature. And sometimes it may just be an enzyme, protein or DNA alteration." Ivey waved her leather arm back toward the Oolahan sanctuary. "Sometimes we need to bring them here to our labs and test the effect of the intervention before we can release the creature again. It takes time. So much time, so many interventions." Ivey's eyes flashed and glittered, the tendrils in Bonnie's mind darkening ominously.

"I must admit, we have never seen a species as avaricious and blood-thirsty as yours. It is an additional sadness that you evolved from our own DNA. The Womb was quite correct. It was a devastating mistake. But we are only Oolahans. We sometimes make errors. Such is the way. But we have learned from them. Something the human race has never developed the capability to do."

Bonnie felt herself mesmerized by the gold glowing nature of Ivey's eyes. Her thoughts raced, ignoring Ivy's thought words. *A navigator—could she . . .?*

"And yes. I am a female."

Bonnie scrambled around so that she was sitting on her knees, her hands supporting her at her sides resting in the thick grass. Her breaking heart began to rocket with the faith that had spread unbidden into her breast spreading like a wildfire.

"Ivey, you said you map pathways. Does that mean you can always find your way back?"

Ivey rolled her radiant eyes. "Sister, why could my duties possibly interest you more than in passing? I can see right into your emotions which I find quite unstable at the moment. I don't know why but I was drawn to you the moment I laid my eyes on you. I think it may have something to do with the fact that you reek of anger, yet great sadness and pain have possession of you."

"Bonnie . . . my name is Bonnie. And I think I can use your help." Bonnie smiled for the first time since landing on Oolaha. Her spirits took flight so high she didn't think she would come down until Peter stood in front of her.

"Sister Bonnie, I am sorry for your great sadness but my dedication is to my calling in the service of the Womb. I am unavailable for help as you suggest. Perhaps one of my Brothers or Sisters can be of service . . ."

"No . . . I need *you*. You're a navigator; *only you*." Bonnie's face paled, blood draining as fast as her spirits had risen. Her voice rose and before she realized it, she was screaming. Ivey scooted back closer to the dome.

From the corner of Bonnie's eye she caught movement. It was coming from inside the dome. Her mind registered the slight motion and dismissed it, her thoughts firmly on how to persuade Ivey to help her.

Ivey stood and prepared to leave. "I am sorry, Sister. I must get back to my duties. I have much to complete today. I wish you well." Ivey bowed. "The Womb be with you."

A faint buzzing filled the air as a tiny pellet flitted from the dome toward Ivey. Glancing inside the dome, Bonnie saw a great scrambling as the creatures that kept it clean rushed to the dome's wall and peered out, their golden eyes wide in the tiny faces that pressed up against the dome wall in dismayed horror.

Ivey's face turned to a study in terror as her fur stood on end. She crouched low, frozen as the bee-like pellet landed on Ivey's crinkled leather arm.

Without a thought, Bonnie reached for the Bible and slapped it against Ivey's arm, flattening the invader. The minion collapsed as if in a faint. Her butterfly jerked up into the air as if on a string.

Ivey's back arched. Glittering fluid began to flow from her nose. A thick viscous liquid, golden in hue began to drip from her ears. Soon her fur was soaked and matted. Before Bonnie's eyes, she watched as Ivey's form began to shrivel and collapse in upon itself.

Glancing up, Bonnie saw a dark line flying toward them from the fortress. As it grew in size, Bonnie could see it was hundreds of minions; Forbation and a few others in the lead. When Forbation landed, he motioned frantically to two others who rushed to Ivey's side. A syringe emerged in the hand of a minion attending Ivey. Quickly, it was inserted into her arm. Another two inserted a tube in her other arm. Golden fluid that flowed from a tank down the tube operated by two more minions completed the tableau.

Forbation's antlers split open. Bonnie watched a red projectile detached from the emulsion it floated in to take to the air. It flew straight to the Bible where the invader lay stunned and broken. It rested on the invader as two minions carefully approached, long metal tongs in their hands, a strange box attached at the end.

Bonnie's hands massaged her pounding temples as she was assailed with disturbing images of dissected and shriveled minions, swirls of darkness overcoming her as she dropped to her knees.

Forbation turned on Bonnie, his golden eyes like slits, hand raised and shaking. "You do not belong here, human. I wish the Womb would ship you all back to your own planet." Forbation laughed bitterly in Bonnie's head. "But we all know how that turned out, didn't we?"

"No, Brother."

Forbation and Bonnie turned to see Ivey struggling to sit, her thin arms held out in supplication as life-giving fluids were pumped into her. Her body had taken on a more robust bulk, the ministrations of her fellow minions a miracle.

"No, Brother Forbation. The human Sister had nothing to do with it. She saved me."

Bonnie's head ached with the competing swirls in her brain. She held up one hand in surrender, the other supporting her forehead. "Please . . . you're hurting me."

Ivey lay back down, her reserves exhausted. Gentle hands held her down as they finished reviving her precious life fluids with their medical support. Forbation rushed to her side. They stared at one another for several minutes. It ended when Forbation nodded his head to the rest of the waiting minions. A collective sigh was heard in Bonnie's brain.

As Bonnie watched, the minions took turns wobbling up to Ivey to touch her face. They then gave their wings a shake and took to the sky to head back to what they'd been doing before the emergency.

It wasn't long before the remaining minions packed everything away, being extra cautious with the tiny invader that sat securely in the box guarded by Forbation's implant projectile.

Backing away from what little remained of the crowd around

Ivey, they took to the air with their burden. Bonnie's eye followed them until she could see them no longer.

"What just happened, Forbation?" Her face screwed up with consternation. An aura glinted in her brain, gentler . . . calmer.

"Please forgive my outburst, Sister. But if you had not been disobeying our directives to not wander around, Ivey would not have come looking for you and would have avoided this danger." Forbation signaled with his hand. The rest of the minions completed their rescue, packed away their equipment and took to the air, Ivey supported between two of them.

"Will she be alright?" Bonnie asked, her voice shaking with fright and the humiliation of her responsibility.

"Yes," replied Forbation. "Fortunately she wasn't too far away for us to save her." Forbation turned to glare at the tiny eyes that still peered with terror through the dome. "This shouldn't have happened at all." The furry golden-eyed creatures that maintained the interior of the dome raced back to their hanging homes at the top of the dome, severely chastised by Forbation.

Turning to Bonnie, he explained. "They know better. It's their job to maintain the stasis inside the domes. I don't understand how they let a rencet through." Forbation's aura darkened. "I'm sure it had something to do with their attention being distracted by one of our new guests," he claimed in a pointed tone. Bonnie ignored his rebuke.

"What exactly is a *rencet*?" she asked.

Forbation aura was angry and raw. "Only the deadliest and most insidious creature known to Oolahans. We thought they had been eradicated decades ago. They are deadly poisonous to most living species, especially minions. They were part of a sorely needed intervention. But when the minions left their planet, the Kreyven had accidently left the portal link intact, just a fraction of a hole. Not enough to do any damage. So we thought . . . We have no idea how many rencets escaped. They can no longer breed, of course. We took care of that before we left their planet. Now the other indigenous life forms on their planet have a fighting chance. Long before now, the rencets would have all died out. Unfortunately, the passing through the portal and visits to who knows where, this side of the solar system, has rendered them either invulnerable or forever enduring." Forbation scratched his forehead in consternation. "We will get to the bottom of this mystery in our labs."

Bonnie stood to return to her quarters. A final blast from Forbation reminded her she was just a visitor.

"Do not come out here again, Sister. Something unstoppable may happen to you next time. The staging areas at the portals are not safe. You should not have come here."

Bonnie cast her eyes down in shame but the bitterness of her words sounded crystal clear. "I am looking for my husband. No one wants to help me. So I'll do it myself."

Forbation puffed up in consternation. "Please don't make me regret leaving you free. This is not the portal through which you arrived." He swept his hands from horizon to horizon. "Look at all the portals. Your simplistic carelessness almost cost us one of our most valuable navigators."

Bonnie lifted her head to scan the panorama in front of her. Portals littered the landscape as far as her eye could see. Letting the number of portals sink in, her heart sank. Her busy eyes frantically tried to identify one over the others.

"They all look the same . . ."

"Well, they're *not,* I can assure you."

Bonnie slowly turned to Forbation. "Which one is the portal we emerged from?"

The Elder minion stared at her unblinking. Not a single twinge of an aura filled her mind. He gave a final defined blink of his large, glowing eyes and took flight. Within seconds he was aloft and on his way back to the minion refuge, leaving the disheveled Bonnie to lug her exhausted body back to the survivors' quarters in disgrace.

For she knew, if one minion knew of her thoughtlessness, they all did, including the Womb.

# Chapter 8

Abby and Cobby walked behind the rest of the survivors as they made their way back to their quarters from the memorial service for their loved ones and friends who had perished with the destruction of Earth. Dried trails of tears left evidence on their drawn and somber complexions.

Dezi had wanted to read from his Bible but Netty had convinced him to leave it behind under the circumstances. After all, the Womb was their host; no longer a theory or far-removed esoteric figure of the truth of their existence and evolution.

Cobby's fingers brushed Abby's. Her head didn't move, her eyes remained forward but she allowed the faint trace of a secret smile to light them up with love for the father of her growing child.

"I'm scheduled for my check-up in a few minutes. I guess I'm the last one to go." Abby nodded her head and cleared her throat, her efforts at normalcy slipping as her wings gave a subtle flex of nervousness.

"I don't think Bonnie has gone yet. Maybe you could try to get her to go with you?" She glanced ahead of them to locate Jose walking with Wil, their heads together in animated conversation, his back still turned toward them. Risking a longing look at Cobby, she felt his finger entwine with hers. He gave her a squeeze of reassurance and support.

"Okay, I'll see what I can do. And you? Are you ready to confront Netty?" She squeezed back.

"Yes, my love. I don't think I can go on with this charade a moment longer. I want to shout to the moon and be in your arms as much as possible. Netty knows something's up. I can see it in her eyes. But she's giving me the time to hear me out." Her eyes gleamed unmistakably. "We need her approval. Wish me luck."

Cobby's darkly handsome face, replete with the wisdom of all of his one hundred and forty years melted her heart. "Ab, just remember

. . . she doesn't own you."

Abby's smile left her lips. "Try to understand. Cob. I have a responsibility and it includes Jose as my mate. There are ramifications we may not be foreseeing. And there is the fact that I will outlive you. And our child, I'm scared about the fact that it may be . . . well . . . different."

"Shhh, let me worry about those things. Chloe's baby will be here in a few weeks or so. She's in the same situation. And no one seemed to care that Scotty was an Elder and she wasn't."

"Yes, but the important difference is that the mother of Chloe's child isn't an Elder. Our child's mother is. There is a big difference between female Elders and males."

Cobby made a face. "It can't be that bad. You all look the same except for the antlers the males don't have. Netty ever tell you what the difference is?"

"A little. Just that the males were eliminated from holding the reins of power—our antlers—because of their human heritage. The Womb doesn't trust the male of our species, neither human nor Elder. She didn't go into much more than that."

Cobby glanced down the corridor to see that the rest of the survivors had moved far in front of them. He pulled on Abby, hanging them back even further. His voice rose.

"This child will be the best of both of us. No matter what happens or what combination of traits the baby inherits, it will be *our* baby. What more could we ask for?" His hand was sliding up her arm. She could feel the tension and passion of his words as the tendons in his hand contracted.

She quickly threw her arms around his neck and thrust her body hard against his. Her wings blocked them from view as she shuddered against him and whispered, "I love you." She released him just as quickly as she heard a plaintive cry.

"Abby . . . can you hurry on up here?" Jose voiced his impatience from down the corridor and in a flash she was gone, leaving Cobby with empty arms and an aching heart.

Hurrying after the beautiful Elder for whom he had such feelings, he managed to catch a glimpse of her shimmering wings as she entered the survivors' quarters. Unfortunately, it looked like Jose's wings alongside hers.

As he entered the quarters, he risked a casual glance as Abby moved to approach Netty, Jose's restraining arm wrapped firmly around hers. He watched as she tugged hard to disengage. Reining in his anger, he moved in their direction. A restraining hand clamped down on him. "Easy, man. This isn't the time. Let her handle it."

Cobby turned to confront the sympathetic frown of Wil whose lion-like tail stood high in the air in support for his friend. Cobby released the breath he'd been holding in with a frustrated whistle. He ran his rough hand over his mouth, feeling the bristle of his growing whiskers. His muscles contracted with stress under Wil's hand.

"What are you talking about, Wil?" He couldn't stop himself from flicking his eyes toward Jose and Abby.

"You know exactly what I'm talking about, man. Stop making it so obvious. They need to sort this out without your interference. It's between the two of them."

Cobby turned on Wil with gruff irony. "You mean the two of them and *my* baby. I think that counts for some say in this, don't you?"

Wil's jaw dropped, his golden eyes flashing. "Your baby? What the heck are . . . no . . . you don't mean." Wil's voice croaked in fearful strains as a shy smile spread across Cobby's face, pride and hope taking root in his eyes.

"Oh boy. This changes everything." Wil quickly pulled Cobby into an alcove. Glancing back, they watched as Netty approached the quarreling Jose and Abby, steering them down a hallway where they vanished.

Wil turned to Cobby with a shake of his head and a mournful proclamation. "You are in for one shit storm now, buddy. I would have thought you'd have better sense than to begin an affair right now."

With a start, Cobby set him straight. "You know me better than that, Wil. This isn't an affair. I've been in love with Abby since the first day I laid eyes on her. With Jose in the picture, it just wasn't to be. She was too young at the time anyway." Cobby continued to share the details of the plans Abby had made with him. He held his breath, hoping for a solution from Wil but it wasn't to be.

Wil agreed; it was all up to Netty now.

Jose sat in the wooden armchair facing Netty and Abby. His wings vibrated noticeably as his clenched teeth kept him from crying out at the pain from his fingernails that dug deeply into the palm of his hands. His face was stiff and wooden.

Abby shed tears as her faltering words sent arrows of hurt and bewilderment into Jose's heart. Netty listened quietly, her face a cypher.

"This is not how I wanted you to find out, Jose. I wanted to talk to Netty alone first."

"You don't think you owed me an explanation first? Give me a chance?" Jose spewed indignation. Abby cast her eyes down.

"It's beyond that, Jose. It's just . . . I . . . I mean we . . ." She cast a quick glance at Netty. "It's part of growing up, Jose. People change."

Jose snorted. "We're Elders. What can he offer you?" His question was met with a silence that vibrated like balloons ready to burst. "What else are you hiding from me, Abby?" Jose glanced over at Netty. "Do you mind? Can we have some privacy here, please?"

After first glancing at Abby, Netty made to rise.

"I'm pregnant, Jose." The words were said in a whisper. But the pride and joy in Abby's voice said everything. Jose turned white. His frame began to shake. His mouth opened then closed. She placed her arm on his.

"I'm so sorry, Jose. You know I will always be there for you. We've been through so much together. You'll always have a place in my heart. I hope we can get through this and still be important to each other."

"You bitch. You treacherous bitch." Reaching out with his trembling hand, he slapped her hard across the face. Abby's hand flew to her face, stunned. Blood drained from her face to expose the perfect print of Jose's hand on her cheek.

"*That's it*, Jose." Netty took a firm hold of his arm and ushered him toward the door where they were confronted by Baby.

"Sister . . . Brother. We can have none of this here. Violence is prohibited. You must leave now. It is against the law of the Womb."

"I think I can handle this." From behind Baby came the stooped figure of Forbation. "No need to let this get out of hand." He looked around the room. "Come with me, Jose . . . please."

Jose ground his teeth, veins on his forehead throbbed. All eyes were on him as his expression went blank. A sigh of relief was palpable as Jose smiled. His eyes lost the dangerous glitter.

"Of course, Forbation." Jose rose quickly and shook out his wings, turning to Abby. "I wish you much luck." A half-bow followed then he glided out of the room with Forbation.

Silence greeted his departure. A gentle stroke announced Baby's presence in Abby and Netty's mind.

"Mark my words, my Sisters. We have not heard the last of this matter with Brother Jose."

Abby and Netty exchanged heavy glances, their relief beginning to dissipate.

"Don't be silly, my little golden worrywart." Netty bent down to scoop up the minion she loved as much as she loved her daughter, Maya. "We are family. This might take some time for Jose to accept but he will come around. Brother Forbation will see to it." She turned to Abby with Baby ensconced firmly on her hip. "The child you are carrying is another matter. We will just need to wait until Chloe has her baby. It should give us a guideline. We will give Jose some time before you and Cobby announce this . . . new beginning. Does that sound fair?"

"Yes, of course, Netty," Abby hastened to reassure her. "We've waited this long, what's a few more days or weeks?"

The three golden creatures reached out to embrace one another, Jose completely forgotten as the prospect of new life swept everything from their minds. Baby flapped his leather legs at Netty's waist as he savored the excitement and the delight of another child on the way.

Forbation hastened Jose away from the survivors' quarters.

"Slow down, Brother. What's the rush?"

Forbation stopped in his tracks and whipped his head around to study Jose, surprised at his peevish and surly tone. "I sincerely hope I do not have trouble brewing here, Brother Jose. You have responsibilities to everyone on this planet."

Jose laughed, his tone incredulous. "I don't have any responsibilities to anyone. I do what I please and when I please."

Forbation froze to gaze into Jose's flashing eyes. Seconds ticked by before Jose heard a grinding.

"I am sorry to hear you say that," intoned Forbation. The wall beside him opened up and out thrust a Kreyven. The hallway was filled with its unmistakable spicy lemon odor. Before Jose could move, the Kreyven struck. It hung high in the air over Jose swaying from wall to wall, then descended like a snake, wrapping its now noxious fumes around the hapless Elder, his wings crushed tightly in its coils.

"Hey . . . Brother Forbation. Make it stop."

Forbation remained silent. The Kreyven increased its pressure, its considerable mass mounting and swallowing Jose's body, leaving only his golden head with its flashing eyes exposed.

"Forbation!"

A dog barked. As it grew closer, Jose recognized the curly white face of Barney, followed by an agitated Echo. "Hey girl . . . *Echo . . . help!*" Jose screamed, plaintively.

Echo's aura stabbed wildly. "Brother Forbation, what is the meaning of this? Brother Jose is part of our family."

Forbation's aura struck back, calm and resolute. "It grieves me, my Sister, but the rules have been broken. I'm sure you have absorbed the details. It is no longer safe for Sister Abby if Brother Jose is free to do as he pleases. The Womb is proven correct again. The male of this species is not to be trusted. If it were not for the fact that he is an Elder . . ."

Echo hung her head.

"What's going *on,* Echo? Can you get me down from here?" shouted Jose.

Echo waddled over to stand unflinchingly in front of the house Kreyven. "Do not worry, Brother. I will stand for you in your trial."

"Trial? What the heck are you talking about? Get me out of this mess." Jose struggled against the Kreyven.

"Please, Brother Jose. Do not fight the Kreyven. It has orders. You will go to another part of the Womb while the trial commences. The Womb will decide what to do with you. I will argue for a position in the labs, something befitting your station."

The Kreyven began to withdraw into the translucent wall of the Womb. "Stay calm, my Brother. I will make sure you are fine." Echo hopped from foot to foot as Jose disappeared with the Kreyven.

Forbation moved forward to place a reassuring hand on Echo's shoulder. Barney stood sniffing at the organic wall; a low whine testified to his distress.

"You know something like this was bound to happen. They can't help themselves. You agreed to these measures before the decision to move them here was made," Forbation admonished Echo. "We will do what we can, but please . . . don't make this worse. His violence may just be related to his dispute with Sister Abby but you know he must be segregated for observation."

The two minions turned to walk arm-in-arm down the hallway, the organic walls beating subtly with their every step.

"This will be quick. I will find something suitable for him." Forbation shook his head from side to side, his disappointment keen. "I just did not think the first to break would be an Elder."

Bonnie lay on her colorful bed staring up at the high ceiling. Squinting her eyes tightly, she thought she could see the ceiling move with the beats of her own heart. Hud sat quietly in a chair by the bedside, finding comfort in her company. Like most men, he found quiet easier to deal with.

"Why won't you help me, Hud? How can you turn your back on Ginger Mae?"

"I'm not turning my back on her, Bonnie. There's just nothing I can do. What do you want from me? Do you want me to go back into the portal with you? That's only going to get us killed." A tear slipped down Hud's face. He wiped it away quickly with the back of his fist as he stood. His handsome world-weary face looked down on Bonnie, his shell-shocked eyes appraising her.

"You need to do your mourning and make your peace. Stop torturing yourself."

Bonnie remained silent.

"Come on. Why don't you come with me? The rest of the women are in the nursery with the babies. With *your* baby. He needs to see his mama. And Forbation wants to meet us after we eat. He has an announcement for us."

"I'll be there. Just not yet."

"Okay, I'll just head down to the nursery to give your son a look-see for you." He bent down and gave Bonnie's arm a squeeze. "See ya later. You *are* planning on joining us for chow aren't you?"

"I'll think about it, Hud."

Nodding his head, the big, sad man left the room.

It didn't take long before Bonnie heard another noise. She sighed to herself with frustration. *Never a moment's peace.* She closed her eyes to feign sleep. Suddenly she felt a finger trace the contours of her face, slowly . . . tentatively.

Her eyes flew open to confront a minion with a disarmingly beautiful fire butterfly attached to her antlers. *Ivey.* Bonnie stared at the minion who stared back. Seconds passed as she wondered why the minion was here.

"You look good, Ivey. Are you healed?"

"Yes, Sister Bonnie, I am."

Bonnie waited for more. Ivey remained silent as she carefully watched Bonnie. Finally the swirling auras in her brain engaged.

"Brother Baby and Sister Echo feel love for their humans. Do you feel love?"

"Why yes, Ivey," she replied, startled and amused by the question. "Do you love someone?"

"No," Ivey replied. "I love no one. Whom do *you* love?"

Taken aback, Bonnie searched her heart. "I love all of my people. We all love one another. And I love Baby and Echo and Tobi and Caesar and all of the animals that came with us from Earth."

"Then why are you so sad? Brother and Sister said there is great joy in loving. I see no great joy in you. I find my joy in my duty just like every minion. But Brother and Sister have something else. Something they call complete happiness. I do not feel that."

"You must be just like me, only sadder. I don't think you have complete happiness."

Ivey wrinkled her nose. "You smell bad."

Bonnie bristled. "I don't have complete happiness because my husband is missing. I told you about that, before the thing from the portal tried to sting you. Remember? I love him more than anything and anyone in the world. And if you don't like how I smell, you can leave."

Ivey looked long and hard at Bonnie. Her butterfly's wings flapped languid trailing lines of firelight over her golden fur. Ivey blinked her mesmerizing eyes. Her fur bristled. "I will leave." She turned to leave Bonnie's bedroom, the fire butterfly sucking greedily from her antlers, content and secure.

Bonnie picked morosely at the cake Dezi had made for the end of dinner. Echo sat along the wall with Barney and Chloe's dog Teddy, happily feeding them pieces of cake while Baby watched, a puppy tucked under one skinny arm and flapping his elongated fingers in the air with consternation over the disappearing cake. *I see not much has changed for Baby.*

She saw that a nooglet had joined the group, Barney warily tolerating his rival. Looking to the other side of the room, Abby and Cobby sat with Wil and Netty; Hud and Kane helped Dezi with the dishes, and Kenya played on the floor with her baby and a laughing Maya, the little girl still unable to control her thrashing tail and drooping wings. Maya gallivanted around, begging for constant attention as usual. She could hardly blame the child after being cooped up for so many years with Father Garcia and the babies, unable to have playmates to develop natural social skills. If she was precocious for her age, the adults certainly took pains to humor her.

A cloudy veil of sorrow descended over Bonnie as she recounted the many changes Maya had been forced to witness in the last year or so since they'd ascended from the Hive and begun to build their new life above on Earth. Her hand to her mouth, she stifled a sob. *And now another different life to live . . .* She wished she could be more like Daisy. Unemotional and committed to her calling. She noted Daisy's absence. *Probably talking to some alien rocks somewhere.*

She wondered where Jose was and who might be taking care of her baby. She found she still wasn't hungry but had taken pains to clean herself up and wash her hair, now swept up in a ponytail out of her way. She discreetly sniffed herself. A faint odor of vomit still clung relentlessly. *Oh well . . . I'll get some new clothes soon.*

"Hi doll. How ya doin'?" Dezi slid into place next to her. Bonnie swallowed and shook her head, afraid to talk for fear of breaking down. Dezi reached out to give her a hug.

"I know it's just not the same with Peter and Ginger Mae gone." Dezi's mournful tone was heartfelt. "I sure miss then. Especially Ginger Mae. She was the best."

Bonnie looked up, her face deliberately alive and determined. "Will you help me, Dezi? We can find them. I know we can. We just need to make someone listen. I have all kinds of ideas. We . . ."

Dezi placed his hand down on hers. "They're gone, hon. You need to accept that." One tear slid down her cheek.

"No, not you too, Dez."

Before Dezi could reply, Forbation walked into the room accompanied by a small group of minions who wore red ribbons hanging loosely around their necks. The room descended into silence as Forbation's aura swirled in their minds.

"It is time for my Brothers and Sisters to begin a new chapter in their lives." He swept his arm back to the waiting minions. "Each of you will be assigned a guide to begin your introduction to the other parts of the Womb. As you tour our facility, I am hoping you will discover a department that will interest you. We need to find your calling."

A whispering buzz went around the room as the survivors wondered at Forbation's pronouncement. Many couldn't wait to see the magic of the Womb and others were excited to learn something new that might give them a rewarding life as the last of the survivors from the vanquished planet Earth.

Forbation began again. "Most of you will notice Jose and Daisy's absence. Jose will not be joining you for some time. He is being kept busy and content, I am happy to report. He will rejoin you when we feel his . . . attitude . . . has mended. And our magnificent wunderkind, Daisy, will rejoin us in about a week. She is off on her first mission with a cadre of minions. This will be her first chance to explore a new civilization in person and utilize her new communication skills. They left through a portal last night."

Forbation smiled and bowed at the various surprised expressions. "I think it is time to begin the tours." He swept his arm toward the door. "Shall we?"

One by one, the survivors stood, a myriad of emotions waltzing across their faces: hesitation, anticipation, fear and duty. Excitedly, they joined Forbation and his team of minions to take their first step into their futures.

# Chapter 9

Jose sat stewing in a tiny room somewhere far from the survivors' quarters. Echo had left a few hours ago, instructing him to get rest, her fire butterfly trailing gay sparks of light behind her.

He scoffed at the overly sensitive nature of the minions. *You'd think Echo would get it after living with us for so long. Especially after the debacle with the Kane, Emma and Elias love triangle so many long decades ago. Shit happens, people change . . . well I haven't changed.* Ironically, Jose glossed over the similarity in his own predicament and the one that had wrought such disaster in the Hive so long ago and so tragically with Emma and Elias.

*These minions just don't understand humans.* Now, he was relegated to this boring room. He surveyed his new quarters, cramped and spare with a bed, a chair and a small table. No opportunity to call a Kreyven for special order comfort items. He eyed the walls with suspicion. Organic as he expected, the throbbing appeared more apparent, more alive in this part of the sanctuary.

As his thoughts turned to Abby and Cobby, he clenched his fists, his knuckles turning white as he squeezed off his blood supply. Shaking his hands to bring back blood, he wondered what he'd done to deserve this betrayal. Hadn't he always gone along with everything Abby wanted? Except now she didn't want him. She wanted the old washed-up yacht jockey. In his anger, he refused to admit that Cobby had been just as instrumental as anyone in their efforts to survive the last century or so.

His face flamed with shame as he remembered standing in front of a black slab of onyx where Forbation and three other minions sat judging him. Echo sitting off to the side, waiting to be called. The four minions at the table conferred, their heads bent together, auras being cast, but Jose found himself unable to understand. At one point, Forbation picked up a red staff and pointed it toward Echo. The trial went on for many minutes but concluded abruptly.

Forbation and the other minions rose and turned their backs to Jose. Without a word, Echo trundled to his side, grasped his hand and tugged until Jose realized the trial was at an end.

Even as he fruitlessly questioned Echo, Jose refused to accept that Forbation and his council had dismissed him so easily. He was an Elder for Pete's sake. *The minions worship Elders, don't they?*

He pounded his pillow in frustration, wondering what would happen next and how long he'd be stuck here. A sound at the door drew his attention. Echo entered, his tiny hand clasped tightly to an apprehensive Abby.

He sprang up from the bed, a relieved smile stretching from ear to ear. "I *knew* you would come, Abby. I just knew it." He swept her into his arms, chatting on and on. "You wouldn't believe what Forbation put me through. How embarrassing. You would think I'd committed a crime." He cringed at the sound of his thoughtless words. He pulled back quickly to look into her face. "Gee, I'm so sorry, Abby. I didn't mean to sound so . . . ."

She pressed her fingers to his lips as she extricated herself from his embrace and moved to the only chair in the room. Echo perched at her feet as they left Jose standing alone with his arms empty. "Sit down, Jose."

He hesitated, unnerved by the tone in her voice. He flopped back down on his bed, turning toward the woman he had loved for so long. Even as his hopes ran high, he ground his back teeth silently. *Yeah, this is the woman that betrayed me for so long.* As he took in her beauty, he wondered for how long and who exactly knew what a cuckold he'd been. Clearing his throat and assuming a bright tone, he asked, "What's up, guys?"

Abby smoothed her smock, her wings hugged tightly to her body and swallowed. "I'm here to explain a few things to you, Jose. Forbation asked me to convey his . . . warm . . . feelings and to let you know where to report in the morning."

Jose sat further back on the bed, stunned. "That's it? His warm feelings?" Jose looked incredulous. "And what about you?" His voice developed an edge. "What about *your* warm feelings? Or do you save them for when you're fucking someone behind my back?"

Abby stood swiftly, the pain on her face infused in her words. "I didn't come here to fight, Jose. If that's what you have in mind, we'll leave."

He raised his hands in supplication. "All right. Please . . . sit back down and tell me why Forbation sent you, of all people." He let loose a bitter laugh. "Does this mean he trusts me?"

Abby sat down slowly, her voice faltering. "I don't rightly know what Forbation thinks. I volunteered." Her voice slowed. "I want to . . . to . . . apologize."

Jose forced a vapid smile to his lips, the pressure from his grinding teeth a welcome tonic. His golden eyes generated a laser glint, brighter than any seen before.

"But my love . . ." the words came out like honey, soft, pliant and sweet, "I'm the one that should apologize. I had no business raising a hand to you. It was just the . . . the shock . . . of hearing of your impending . . ." His eyes pointedly lingered on her abdomen. Unconsciously, her hand went to her belly protectively.

"Well, yes . . . erm . . ." With a self-conscious gesture, she adjusted her hair. "I guess that is understandable. You should have been the first to know. Cobby and I . . ."

"*Please*. Don't even think of mentioning that bastard's name in my presence." Jose tried to suppress the bile from his voice. He stood up from the bed and advanced toward her. He could see her shrink from him. Reining himself in, he extended his arms, a gesture warm and friendly, a fresh grin on his face. "Are you happy? Do you feel well? In your condition . . . you're not a spring chicken, after all."

Abby relaxed a sigh of relief and hope lit her face. She rose to meet his embrace. "You know I will always love you, Jose."

"And I *you*, Abby. I'm here, if and when you need me. I'll always be here." He looked around the room. "Well, not *here* . . . but you know what I mean."

She glanced up into his face. "Then you really do understand?"

"Understand what?"

She glanced down at her feet. "You know . . . about us. Falling out of love . . ." She returned to his face. "It was bound to happen, you know. We were just kids." She smiled, gently. "My first love. It was only natural that we would cling to one another, under the circumstances." Pain radiated across her face. "So much horror, so much death." She laid her head on his shoulder as he held her tight, gripping her back.

"Shhh, shhhh. It's okay." He bit down, the pain from his tongue helping him to think straight. "Everything will work out just fine. By the way, did Forbation say anything to you about me? Can I come back now?"

Her eyes looked sorrowful. "I'm afraid not, Jose." He tasted the saltiness of his own blood as he bit harder.

"I was told to tell you a minion will fetch you in the morning. We're all getting a tour to help us decide where we will best fit."

He gave her hand a squeeze. "Well then . . . I'll see you tomorrow on the tour."

As they reached the door, they were confronted by an amazing sight. Hovering in the air on a chair was a disheveled Chloe. Alongside her transport floated a trio of minions with dozens of fluffy white nooglets fluttering above, their comically vicious canine faces anxious not to miss a thing. Golden light waltzed with every color of the spectrum and flooded the huge hallway.

"What the heck?" exclaimed Abby, her hand to her mouth in laughter.

"You can put me down now, boys." Chloe's eyes were wide with trepidation and mirth. Underneath the platform where Chloe's chair rested was a smaller version of the anti-gravitational device the minions used on the spheres that held the aliens captured on other planets as they emerged from the portals.

"Boys, can you please put me down?" They moved to accommodate. "Yes, thank you . . . thank you." Chloe breathed deeply, her relief palpable. Cupping her arm around her enormous belly, she gingerly stood up from the chair and stepped off the platform. She nodded her head gratefully as the minions lowered the device to the floor and backed away to find a spot to wait, sitting with legs crossed and backs touching, faces looking at Chloe in worship.

"They really like me. Isn't that cute?" announced Chloe, pride and wonder mixing with amazement. "Let's go inside."

Jose rushed to Chloe's side, his arms outstretched to help her walk. Over his shoulder he cast one last glance at Abby who enclosed herself in her wings and disappeared.

Chloe patted him softly on the arm. "Come on, Jose. She's gone." Together they entered Jose's room, ensconcing Chloe on the bed where she curled up. Making room on the bed, she directed him to join her.

He sighed deeply, making himself comfortable. "So I guess you heard?"

She rolled her eyes. "The minute you slapped Abby, everyone knew. They're linked mentally, you know. They each know everything as soon as another forms a thought. You know how it works. If you and Abby thought you could keep anything a secret here, you're crazy. You might as well know they've all known about the baby since we got here."

Jose ran his hand through his unkempt hair. "Well, isn't that just ducky?"

"Come on, Jose. You must have had an idea. All this time and you never knew Cobby had something for Abby?"

He shook his head. "Great . . . that makes it even worse, kiddo." Jose propped his chin up with his hand. "How convenient Karen just happened to not make into the portal. I don't recall seeing her that morning, do you?"

Chloe startled, not wanting to share what she knew about Karen from the story given to her by Kenya the morning they'd found her dead in the bathing cave. *No sense giving Jose more to chew on and rile himself up over.*

"No, I didn't see her," she declared. "I'm not trying to make you feel bad, Jose. I just want you to face facts so you can get on with your life. We have so much uncertainty in our lives as it is. I was hoping you might find a purpose working here with the Oolahans." She smiled shyly, rubbing her belly. "And I know a little someone that is just dying to meet his uncle." Her eyes welled up with glistening tears. "It might make up for what we missed when we were little. I can't even remember Mama and Papa."

Jose smiled, his eyes far way.

Her face crumbled, her voice broken. "And Scotty . . . my Scotty."

Laying her head down on the pillow, she sobbed. Jose waited until she cried herself out, his hand rubbing her back to quietly let her know he understood. Her sobs stopping, Chloe punched the pillow and sat up, her complexion wan, but her eyes flashing.

"Sorry . . . I just can't seem to stop myself. I thought I was all cried out." She wiped her eyes with the sleeve of her smock. "I just can't help wondering if things would have turned out differently if Echo had been with us instead of flying off with the nooglets without a word to anyone. Barney wouldn't have run away and we wouldn't have been caught out in that field for the flamer to find. If . . . if . . . if." She clenched her fist. "It's entirely the Womb's fault," she stated resentfully.

Jerking her head up, she clasped a hand to her mouth and looked around quickly. "I didn't mean that, Jose." Tears began to slip from her eyes again. "I'm sorry . . . the Womb has been good to us and I'm very grateful. It's just . . . ."

He took his sister into his arms. "Shhhh . . . I understand, hon. So much has happened. And you're pregnant. That's enough to push anyone off their rocker. I'm sure the Womb will cut you a break. We're all still in mourning. Very little is expected of us right away. Although Forbation seems to have plans for us."

Chloe swiped at her eyes with the back of her hand. "Well, maybe that will help. I'm going to be in the nursery with Maya and the babies but everyone else will start some kind of job. It'll be interesting, I'm sure."

"Have you heard what Abby and Cobby will be doing?" Jose asked innocently.

Chloe gave him a sharp look. "Does it matter right now? You can bet it will be far away from anything Forbation might have *you* do."

"I know where I'll be working. The intake and quarantine labs. Forbation said it's a prestigious position, not without its dangers," he exaggerated.

Giving Jose a deep searching glance, Chloe took a gulp of air. "I can't afford to lose you too, Jose. Please don't do anything foolish." She reached out to clasp his hand in hers. "Promise me."

Jose laughed.

"No, I mean it. I want you to promise me you won't do anything to put yourself or anyone else in jeopardy.

"Okay. I promise." He squeezed her hand. "I know I need to be here for the bambino."

"And for me too, Jose. We *both* will need you. Just because Abby has moved on doesn't mean others don't love and need you." She hugged her brother tight, feeling his arms around her but missing the hard glint in his eyes at the mention of Abby's name.

"Well, I better get back. My entourage awaits." She extended a smile. "I just wanted to check on you."

Slipping off the bed, he helped her waddle to the door.

"I think you could use a house Kreyven here, don't you? Can I send you some more comfortable items? Just in case you're here for a while?"

Jose laughed, the confidence back in his voice. "Don't worry, Chloe. I love you for thinking of me but I won't be here for much longer." He turned to kiss his sister goodnight without the slightest idea how sadly prophetic his flippant words would be.

# Nine Days AE (After Earth)

# Chapter 10

Dezi sat in his seat near the stove, taking a break. He stared at the blank sheets of paper that sat begging on the table in front of him.

"I think you can find a good use for these, my boy," Forbation had said when he plonked the empty sheaves of paper down next to the chartreuse mixture he'd been beating to death with a wooden spoon. He knew he could have worked out a fancy gadget with the help from a home Kreyven and his job would have been easier but Dezi prided himself on the old-fashioned methods from when Salina taught him to cook so long ago on Earth.

"What the heck do ya expect me to do with this pile of paper, Mr. Forbation? Use it in a new recipe?"

Forbation's aura caressed Dezi's mind, finding delight in the simple, loyal mind of the cocky man. The wise minion raised his head to the shelf Dezi had attached to the wall days ago. There rested the dog-eared copy of the *Holy Bible* that he found to be most useful only as ancient fables from a forgotten past.

Dezi followed Forbation's gaze. "You have an objection to the last known book from Earth, Mr. Forbation?"

The wise minion winced. "*Brother* Forbation, if you don't mind, Brother Dezi. As to the book . . . I am not as offended as you most likely think. I admire any artifact from a lost civilization."

Dezi's face darkened with blood. "Lost civilization? Last time I looked we were all here for breakfast and none of us are lost. We just live in a new location, that all. With all due respect, Mr. Forbation, I trust you not to use those words around any of my family if ya please."

Silence ticked by slowly as Dezi waited for an aura in response. Forbation cocked his head and stared into Dezi's face. He raised a golden, crinkled hand and caressed the blank and crisp papers on the table. He nodded his head a few times and smiled at Dezi. Without sending another aura, he calmly patted the paper and left the kitchen, his wings clasped tightly to his back and his lion-like tail held high.

*What the heck was that all about?* Dezi wondered.

"Hey, Dez," Cobby shouted from the kitchen entrance. He was shadowed closely by Abby.

Dezi looked up. *They certainly have been thick as thieves lately.* "What's up guys?"

The couple hurried over, Cobby dropping a small, slender amber metal cylinder on the sheaf of paper Dezi had pushed aside. As it landed, it made a mark on the paper.

"What's this, a pen?" Dezi picked up the metal object. It sat in his hand just like a pen. He turned it to and fro, not seeing what end to write with. Quickly dropping it back on the paper, he rubbed his arm as a flush of warmth infused his skin and traveled up to his shoulder.

"What's the matter, Dezi?" asked Abby.

Brushing the strange sensation off, Dezi resorted to his usual bravado. "Nothin' babe. What could be wrong?" He gave Abby his best grin. "We're all alive aren't we?" Turning back to the metal object, he nodded his head toward it. "So what's with that?"

Cobby bent down and picked it up. "It looks like a pen but I don't see where the point is." He glanced at Dezi's blank papers. "It made a mark." He reached down and tried to scribble on the paper. The metal object left no marks.

"So what's the big deal about a pen that doesn't work?" asked Dezi.

I don't *know* if it's a pen, Dezi. Forbation didn't say."

"Forbation?"

"Yeah, He stopped us in the hallway and asked us to pass this on to you." Abby's brows drew tight, furrows on her brow causing her skin to tighten. "He also asked us to make sure you guard it with your life."

Dezi drew back. "What the heck is all the mystery about? Why can't he just tell me straight out what he wants?" Dezi slapped his hand on the paper, causing the cylinder to roll off the table. Cobby caught it before it hit the floor.

"I don't know, Dezi, but I'm sure Forbation has a reason he wants you to have this." Abby slipped her hand over Dezi's.

"He did say one other thing."

"Well, *give,* girl."

"He said you'll be the one to make it happen. You're the one with the recipes." She looked blankly at Dezi. "What do you think he means?"

"Damned if I know." Rising, Dezi slipped the cylinder into his apron, rolling the papers and adding them to his bottomless pockets. "All I know is, ya better not be late for dinner." Dismissing the subject, Dezi rose and headed to his new supply chest. There were chores to be done and dishes to prepare. And if anyone should avoid being late, he knew it was him. Not with this hungry crew on his hands.

As evening wore on, Bonnie helped Dezi clear the remains of dinner. He was reminded of what they'd all lost as the noise level in the kitchen never rose above a decent decibel level. Quite unlike the tempo and riotous point that had been the norm back on Earth. Forcing the memory of the voices they'd lost from his mind, Dezi listened in to the gentle stories that circulated the table.

Sidestepping a dancing Maya, he showed her back to her mother as he listened to Netty explaining her work to the others. "It was very rudimentary but it was life. My very first original life form." She beamed with pride, reaching down to hug Echo. "We did it together. I can't take all the credit."

"So where was Wil in all this?" asked Cobby. Abby gazed fondly at Wil.

"It was Wil that understood that we shouldn't try to create something that fulfilled too many functions. It eats, breathes and can multiply on its own. Yes, its life span is very quick but the original subject still lives after two days. Forbation promised that it will be sent to a sustainable habitat within the next month or so if we can get it to evolve a long lifespan. It needs some more study and a few more cell generations before it can be released. Just in case. We need to know everything about it. How it will survive, its limitations, its breeding capacity. Then we watch closely how it interacts with the new environment and the other life that resides there. We need to be ready to make an adjustment if any deleterious conditions evidence themselves."

From across the table Kenya commented, "It sounds like fun, Netty, but so much responsibility. What if you accidently created a monster?"

"This is being done on a cellular level, hon. It is completely controllable. Although it hasn't always been so. That's how some diseases start. And I have it on good authority that some wondrous life has been created from mistakes." Netty lowered her voice. "Like the Kreyvens . . . and us, Homo sapiens."

"But you were a different kind of mistake, Sister. A mistake to make all minions proud." Echo's aura included them all, suffusing the room with feelings of love and family.

The night wore on as the remaining survivors chatted on. Raucous laughter, Dezi's desserts and war stories about their new jobs all combined to help lift their spirits and give them hope that their lives could go on with satisfaction and comfort as long as they had each other.

The lone dissenter sat back against the wall, careful to not touch the organic membrane that clearly lived, breathing rhythmically as the Womb oversaw their new sanctuary. Bonnie strummed her fingers on the table, torn between frustration and anger. She was learning to keep it buried until the right opportunity came her way. She glanced up briefly, wondering where Jose was. The time was well overdue for him to rejoin the survivors. Her eyes rested on a relaxed and happy Cobby and Abby. They sat chatting with Chloe as Maya strived for their attention, Netty and Wil looking on indulgently. She wondered if the new twosome had something to do with Jose's absence. *I need to start paying attention. Maybe it's time to accept things as they are. Put some pain behind me and join the human race again.* She snorted with bitterness at the inadvertent irony of her thought. Glancing around, she observed Dezi staring at her. She sent him a tentative smile.

Growing bored, she rose and slipped away silently to her bedroom, completely missing Dezi's answering grin and the moment Ivey stopped by shyly to ask for her. When told Bonnie had gone to bed, the vibrant minion quickly flitted away, her proud fire butterfly trailing flames and sparks behind her.

Dezi cut a large piece of his mixed grain and red tulip flatbread. It didn't look appetizing but it tasted like heaven thanks to the red berry-like beads that were cultivated to feed one of the captive species the minions were studying. It had been a great privilege to accompany Baby through the labyrinth hallways as the happy minion's aura plucked away in Dezi's brain, extolling the wondrous nature of their enormous and eclectic growing field.

When they'd finally arrived at their destination a few days ago, Dezi was shocked to see not a drop of soil or the lush greenery he'd expected. Instead, he was met by rows and rows of shelves that featured thousands and thousands of enclosures. Some had plants growing out the top, some featured only an array of what Baby claimed was special agar that fermented the growth of nourishment, indigestible by humans. To Dezi's surprise, a group of minions worked feverishly with tools to pummel what looked like green rocks into stones that were carried off to become delectable delights for another species.

It was within these rows of strange edibles that Baby led him to a deep and low table that contained an enclosure of what resembled nests. On the nests sat dome-shaped creatures about five feet tall. They were covered with black and white scales. Each creature was surrounded by five or six smaller creatures that clamored for attention. The creature's obvious young did not have scales. Red beads hung in clumps from their hides. The table top was littered with them from the offspring that had aged and matured into adolescence.

Baby's aura explained. "We call them tulips." He stretched out his tiny hand and swept up a handful of discarded beads. "It only takes a few to produce a savory flavor and appealing color. Try it tonight, Brother Dezi. You will have a wondrous hit on your hands."

Baby's wings fluttered with excitement, picking his body up off the floor. Settling down, he reached under the table to pull out a sack. Together, they collected a sackful of beads, the previous owners of the flavor beads ignoring them both.

"I should warn you, though. It has a strange effect on certain people. Nothing big. Just . . . gentle. And distinct. You will see, my Brother."

Dezi's eyes swept the room as he wondered what the heck Baby meant. As far as he could see, tables were piled with unusual living plants and mysterious objects that when combined with another strange item would produce a tasty confection for any number of species held captive for study or observation. Minions filtered in and out, harvesting as they went. Everyone needed to be fed regardless of species.

"Will the gang like it, Baby? That's all I care about."

Baby nodded his head, eyes big and gleaming. "Fear not, Brother."

Tapping his chin, Dezi got an idea. It sounded like the beads were special. Something had been percolating in the back of the lonely chef's mind for a few days and the beads might just be the answer.

His mind snapped back to the present moment, as Dezi scanned the kitchen. No one was paying him any attention. He quickly wrapped the fragrant piece of flatbread in a cloth and made his way from the hallway to the bedrooms, stopping in front of a doorway he'd had his eyes on for a few days.

"Hello? Bonnie, mind if I come in?"

Bonnie looked up from her bed with startled eyes. "Well sure, Dez. Come on in," she welcomed him.

Taking a seat, Dezi blinked as he took in the riot of colors and designs. "Yeah, this is what I would expect from you," he said shyly.

Bonnie glanced at him sharply, not missing the change in his behavior. "What's up, Dez?"

Dezi brought his hand with his offering out from behind his back. "This is for you." A breathlessness escaped from his lips, drawing her attention again.

She slipped off the bed to reach out. "You didn't need to do this,

Dez. I'm not really hungry." She ran her hand through her hair, making it stand on end. "As a matter of fact, I'm a little tired. Do ya mind . . . ?"

Dezi's face fell, his hurt so obvious Bonnie relented.

"Ya know, I could always stand for a little more of one of your goodies." She sat back on the bed and leaned in to take a sniff. "I don't think I've tasted this before. It smells great." The flatbread disappeared down her throat. A lazy look appeared in her eyes, a smile dimpled her face. "Come on over here and sit by me, Dez." She patted a spot on the bed. Dezi hurried over and got comfortable on the bed.

"Ahhhh . . . now isn't this luxury?" Bonnie sighed in contentment. Dezi edged deeper in the softness of the bed, Bonnie a mere three inches from him.

"So how come we haven't gotten together like this before? It reminds me of the time we raised Chance. Remember that little devil?" she laughed.

"Yeah. I sure loved that little guy," Dezi grinned.

Bonnie sighed. "We did good together with Chance. I had so much fun with you, Dez. That was soooo long ago. Decades. Before I married Peter." At the mention of Peter's name, Bonnie grew silent. "Dezi . . . he's not coming back is he?"

"No, babe. I don't think he will."

Bonnie gave a shudder, the beginning of a torrent she'd been holding back. Dezi reached out to hold her, wetness soaking his shirt as she cried out the healing tears that might . . . just might . . . start her on the path to recovery. *Maybe it will give me a chance?* He grinned to himself as he realized the pun. He could only hope.

Bending down, he placed a slight kiss on her head and wrapped his arms tighter.

# Chapter 11

Jose hurried along the corridor, its translucent walls throbbing with life as he found his way back to the part of the Womb where his last tour had ended. He attempted to shrug off the tomb-like silence of the place, anxious to hear the laughter and real voices of his friends and family again. Human voices, not voices in his mind.

Forbation stood waiting for him, staff in hand, with other minions flying haphazardly. The day's work had begun in earnest. But quiet . . . always the silence. If he listened hard maybe he would hear the rustling of the minions' wings as they fluttered by. As he approached Forbation, minions began to cluster overhead, preening with the hope that Jose would notice them. He gave them a snappy salute as Forbation waved them back to work with his staff.

"Good morning, Brother Jose. I see you look well." Forbation appeared to study Jose closely. His aura caressed Jose's brain. "I hope we can come to some kind of agreement today. You have seen every inch of the Womb that offers a splendid opportunity to dedicate your life's work."

Jose assumed a petulant scowl. "Well, you won't let me work with Abby and nothing else has grabbed me. You won't let me experiment and I'm not about to clean up after the life forms you have around here. I think I could be more useful than that."

Forbation's aura swirled soundlessly as he studied Jose. Finally he relented. "All right. I will allow you to accompany a group on a tour of the weapons room. Abby, Netty, Wil, Echo and Baby will be along. Perhaps it is time for you to integrate back into your family."

Jose brightened, a disbelieving smile on his face. "Gee . . . thanks Forbation."

Forbation winced. "Brother . . . Brother Forbation, please."

Jose grabbed Forbation and lifted him off the floor to swing him around, his staff clattering to the floor.

"Please, Brother Jose. My bones are not meant for this extreme behavior. Please put me down."

Jose sat him back on the floor, clapping his hands in delight. "Okay, let's get this show on the road."

Forbation unfurled his wings and straightened up. "Come. We have a way to go." He rippled his wings then took to the air, Jose and his larger wings cartwheeling above, followed more slowly. As Forbation and Jose approached the Elders that stood alongside a plain wooden door, Jose's hurt quickly vanished. Landing gingerly, they were greeted by a show of warm hellos. Maya peeked from behind her mother's skirt, tugging on Echo's hand.

Netty's aura spoke to Forbation as she announced to all. "I hope you don't mind me bringing her with us. She's so restless and I thought if I spent some extra time with her . . ."

Forbation patted her arm. "That is quite alright, Sister. But don't let her out of your sight. The objects in these rooms are not toys."

"Look, Mama." Maya held up her other hand to display Echo's long-forgotten fanny pack. "Echo let me have it. If I wear it, I will become a *dude*. Just like Echo used to be."

"*Used* to be?" Echo's indignation resonated.

Netty laughed ruefully. "I'm sure that's what we all need. Watching you turn into a *dude*. Well . . . strap it on and let's go."

Everyone waited while Maya struggled with the fanny pack. Echo stepped up to lengthen the belt. The adults turned away as Netty captured her exuberant child's hand to bring up the rear.

Forbation turned to open the plain wooden door that revealed a wall of a hard substance. He slammed it with his staff, the sound low, and the timber solid. As if a signal had been given, the wall slid back to reveal a vast auditorium lined with every kind of contraption under the sun. Shiny and dull metals, rounded and pointy. Boxed objects of all sizes and against one wall were guns, in rows as long as the eye could see: small guns, large guns, incomprehensible guns and guns pretzeled into phenomenal shapes. No one ever seemed to have any trouble identifying guns. No matter what they looked like, you still needed to point and pull a trigger. In the middle of the floor sat rows of small metal vats of liquid, surrounded by a tightly woven mesh; around and over the top.

"What is this exactly?" Abby asked.

Forbation stepped forward and with a flourish of his hands proclaimed, "This is our weapons lab."

"Weapons? Why do you have need of weapons? You're about *life*."

Forbation's eyes glittered. "Yes, we are. Life is our reason for being. If only other species felt the same way. You see . . . these weapons don't belong to us. They belong to species we have studied in the past. We need to know their strengths and weaknesses."

As Forbation spoke they strolled down into the room, Maya growing impatient for her mother's attention as Netty and Wil's covert looks expressed their concern and trepidation. Gleaming metals and razor edges greeted them everywhere they looked. They remained mystified by the enigma of other displays.

"Follow me. I have arranged a surprise for you." Forbation led them over to a thick metal cube that rose six feet from the floor. Two waiting minions stood at attention as the group approached, their tails twitching anxiously.

"Shh . . . Maya honey . . . settle down," Netty placed her arm on the slender shoulder of her daughter. Forbation tossed a baleful glance at Netty and Maya before continuing.

At a signal from Forbation, the minions drew back and a wall in the cube opened. Inside sat another cube, this one five inches tall. A blast of frigid air wafted out at the Elders. The minions rushed in and placed a solid piece of wood in the farthest corner and ran back to the door to press the button that closed the door. From a concealed control, one of the minions pressed another button and a large panel slid back where the door had been, revealing a window into the cube.

"What are we supposed to see, Brother Forbation?"

The wise minion placed his hands to the sides of his face for emphasis. "You will be witnessing one of the most destructive and insidious weapons ever devised by another species." He held up a finger. Even Maya settled down, feeling the tension from the adults. With a nod to the minions, he commenced the demonstration.

All eyes focused on the small cube inside the big cube. As they watched, the cube grew translucent and fractured, splitting open along the break. An olive-green round object sat up and slithered out over the fractured cube. It was tubular in shape with a glistening eye at the tip of what appeared to be the head.

"It is called a skate."

Like a five-inch cobra, it focused on the block of wood in the far corner of its shared space. And then it vanished. The Elders laughed nervously, glancing at one another as if to ask "Did we see that?"

"Allow me to caution you, my Brother and Sisters. Do *not* take your eyes off the skate."

"But it's gone, Forbation," declared Jose. "There is nothing to keep our eyes on."

Forbation bristled. "Patience and well-trained powers of observation are skills I recommend highly, Brother Jose."

"Look!" shouted Wil. Before the word had fully left his lips, the skate reappeared. It was hanging in the air three feet over the piece of wood. Its head dipped down and what everyone had assumed was its eye detached from the body like a projectile and attached to the wood, sending up a spark of light that promptly blinked out, taking the block of wood with it.

The corner where the wood had stood was now empty. All eye turned to the skate. Where the previous eye had detached sat a brand new eye, milky and new. As they watched, the milkiness disappeared, shed off in a clump of discarded cells to float to the floor.

The skate then turned back on itself and dropped down toward the remains of the cube where it had been housed. Landing on the shards, it curled itself into a ball. The shards reattached and sat as seamlessly as it had been before the disappearance of the stick of wood.

"Huh." Jose turned to Forbation. "Well, that was cool. It made the wood disappear."

Wil rested his hand on Jose's shoulder. "I think there's more to it than that, Jose."

Forbation seemed pleased, though his aura plucked somberly. "Have you not learned that all is never exactly as it seems here in the Womb?"

"The wood didn't just disappear, did it, Brother Forbation?" asked Wil.

"That is correct, Brother Wil. It was actually evaporated. There might be some cells left from the wood that we could locate on the floor but I doubt it. The temperature inside the cube is now high enough to create the energy it would take to power what was known as New York City from your vanquished planet for three hundred years. The power of the skate is immense. We have never been able to completely measure it."

Forbation raised his staff, the signal for several minions that stood by to go into action. They hurried up to the cube with a slender black contraption that sank into the cube. Elaborate tubing of a never-before-seen metal emerged from the contraption.

Jose scoffed. "A book of matches would do the same thing, just take longer."

"That is where you are dead wrong, my Brother." Forbation faced the group. "The skate is quite a weapon. It adjusts its power based on the size and composition of its adversary. Had it been a piece of metal, the spark would have been larger. Had it been a city, we would not be standing here."

Forbation's statement was met with surprise. "A city? The skate has that power?"

Forbation turned to Netty. "Yes, my dear Sister. The skate has the power of all of the bombs that destroyed your planet so long ago all rolled into one . . . and more."

More than one face drained of blood.

"Brother Forbation, isn't it a risk to house it here?"

Forbation smiled, his aura calm and confident. "There is no better place to contain it. We cannot risk it falling into the wrong hands or worse yet, *escape*. It could destroy our planet or any other it found in its line of sight. We discovered a cold environment renders it mostly harmless. It's alive yet not entirely organic. It does not have a brain as we know brains but does respond to electrical and some chemical stimulation. It cannot communicate. It is a very ancient weapon and at one time was controlled by its maker. We do not attempt to control it. Merely subdue it."

He pointed to the minions who held the tubing up to the cube. "We are sucking out the energy for use elsewhere. The frigid atmosphere will re-establish itself and the skate will 'hibernate' until another object crosses its path and dares to challenge it. It only takes a few minutes before the skate is armed again, as you saw."

"Maya, please leave Echo alone." Netty had turned to see her daughter tugging on the hapless minion. She squatted down, her wings lifting high to clear the floor. She clutched her daughter in her arms as the child attempted to squirm away. "This isn't playtime, Maya. Now behave or I will have you taken back to the nursery."

"I don't want to be with the babies," Maya sulked, continuing to twist in her mother's arms.

"Stop. I mean it, young lady."

Wil's arm shot out from nowhere to subdue his truculent daughter. *"That's enough, right now."*

As her father cowed her, Maya stood silent, all of the adults' attention now back with Forbation as he moved them along to another display.

"You will be pleased to see we did not forget the weapons of Earth."

And there they were. Laid out as proudly as any earthly gun collector could dream about. The array was mind-boggling. From the antique long guns, flintlock pistols and infantry rifles to the more modern Glock, Walther, Sig, and Smith & Wesson. Further down the line sat machine guns and torpedoes. Alongside every weapon sat open boxes of ammunition.

"We test them from time to time. They are kept in top-notch condition," Forbation's aura preened.

Jose reached out to examine a little Beretta 3032 semi-automatic pistol. "I bet you wish you had something like this in your pocket way back when, Netty, huh? Perfect for a woman to hide in her apron." Jose aimed the Beretta at a passing minion.

"Jose!" A panic-stricken Abby knocked his hand aside.

"Brother Jose." Forbation's cane struck Jose's hand, knocking the weapon to the ground with a clatter.

Jose stood perplexed, his gun hand cradled, wincing in pain.

"I was just playing, for Pete's sake."

"Who plays with weapons, Jose? Really."

Wil bent over to pick up the Beretta, placing it back on the table to rest alongside its neighbor. "I'm so sorry, Brother Forbation. Your hospitality and heart is immense. But I think we will accept this as the end of our tour. I'm sure you understand."

Forbation bowed at the waist. The crowd moved to the front of the room, Jose's face beet-red.

With the attention off the weapons table, no one noticed Maya snaking her small hand out to lift the Berretta, jam it into her fanny pack, and skip happily back to her mother.


Dezi mopped the floor underneath his work bench. Setting the mop aside, he pulled his stool up to the bench and reached for the paper Forbation had left with him. He turned the pages on what had started out to be general notes and recipes with comments regarding the likes and dislikes of the survivors. It had morphed into a diary of sorts with Dezi jotting down other observations in the kitchen. It was surprising how many secrets and adventures were aired over a hefty slice of sweet pie with its fluffy lemon texture that had been ground from the slender but prolific vines cultivated in the minions' growing field. The vines also made an unbreakable rope when dried and woven together.

Dezi picked up his ink pen and started writing. He shook his head and laughed to himself over the antics from dinner last night. He wondered if Jose was ever going to be allowed back with the rest of them. He almost felt sorry for the poor guy. But you just can't go pulling a gun on someone and threatening to kill them.

And if it hadn't been for Hud, who had liberated the gun from Jose, they might have a dead Cobby on their hands. Dezi wondered if Forbation would have let Cobby die. Or if they had some kind of healing procedure like they had in the Hive back on Earth.

Dezi felt an ache in the back of his abdomen as he thought of Earth. Pushing the yearning aside, he forced himself to continue to write. It was getting late and he wanted to drop in on Bonnie before he went to bed.

He'd seen the navigator minion hanging around earlier. *What was her name . . . IV?* He wondered what the attraction was. He thought he'd seen the minion's fire butterfly leave ribbons of light down the hallway toward the bedrooms.

He looked down on the paper at his childish doodles. He would love it if some day Bonnie would take him seriously. But he knew it would never happen until that last spark about rescuing Peter faded from her mind, and that might take years. He sighed. *That's just the way women are*, he mused, sighing again. Always a groomsman, never a groom.

Ivey stood at the entrance to Bonnie's bedroom, watching as she played with an infant on her bed. The infant crawled toward the edge and Bonnie scooped him up, shaking and tickling until the baby burst with shrieks and laughter, baby blather flooding the room.

"Hello, Ivey. Come on in," shouted Bonnie amid the squeals. "This kid is exhausting me."

Two minion heads peeked around the edges of a chair, ecstatic golden faces that had eyes only for Bonnie and Baby Peter. Bonnie nodded toward her fans. "They're waiting to take the baby back to the nursery. You would think the baby was theirs the way they fuss over it. I can't even *get* into the nursery . . . it's so crammed with minions that want to hold the babies."

Ivey made her way to the bed, her aura casting out to Bonnie. "Do you mind if I touch him?"

"Not you too, Ivy?"

"The babies are special. We don't bring the young of any species here. And we are born fully mature with all memories of our history intact. Our cells contain all the information we need and anything that is missing is supplied by the collective mind of our species. So we have very little exposure to newborns or young. And of course, the babies have come from you. You who are part of us yet very separate. We don't get a chance to establish relationships with our birth parent after we are born. They expire shortly after giving birth. It is more like providing a replacement to continue the missions for the Womb." Ivey's aura slowed. She glanced at Bonnie from underneath her long eyelashes. "You are so mysterious and special to us. We are trying to understand some of your customs." Bonnie covered Baby Peter, snuggling him tightly into the covers as the nursery minions looked on, golden noses inching closer to the baby.

"And what customs are you wondering about, Ivey?"

"Well, I know you are still mourning the Brother you call your husband. If you need a husband, why not just chose another one? I can tell Brother Dezi will be fine with that. He wants you to pick him next. Then you will be happy again."

Bonnie laughed as her cheeks burned. "No Ivey, it doesn't work that way. I'm not in love with Dezi. I mean, I love him but I'm not *in* *love* with him. Do you know what I mean?"

"I'm not sure." Ivey's aura slowed. "What about me? Do you love me? I love you. I loved you the moment I saw you when I was coming in from a mission. Do you remember that, Sister Bonnie?" Bonnie was shocked to silence.

Ivey's aura continued, "You were so sad. I wanted to make you happy. That is love, is it not?"

Bonnie clasped Ivey's hand in hers. "There are many kinds of love," she started slowly. "I love both you and Dezi. You are my friend. But Peter was my husband. It's different."

"Yes, I know. You have intercourse to have babies. You don't want to have intercourse with Dezi?"

Bonnie looked aghast and laughed at the same time. "You are very funny, Ivey. But no. I don't love Dezi the same way I love Peter. Dezi does things for me because we are great friends. Best friends. But that's not enough to build a married life."

"He does things for you? I can do things for you. I will marry you, Sister Bonnie. We can have offspring. I will implant your eggs and give birth for you."

"Oh honey, come here." Bonnie took Ivey into her arms. "I love you for making such a fine offer. But my heart still belongs to Peter. It's the human way. He will always be my first love. Maybe in time I'll get over it but I doubt it. Besides, I don't think an interspecies mating . . . er . . . coupling would be the right way to go here. We are both females by the way. In my race, we mate with a man to have a baby."

"Yes, I know, Sister." The aura whispered the dead serious thoughts of the eager navigator. "But I will check with Forbation." Ivey slid off the bed. "I will tell him of my need and we will make a new rule. I will go find him now." Before Bonnie could dissuade the misguided minion. Ivey wobbled to the door, encountering Dezi, then disappeared.

"Hey, babe. What's up? Dezi strolled into the room, waving to the minions drooling over the baby.

Bonnie fell back on her pillow, looking up at the ceiling. "It looks like I have another problem on my hands. Turns out Ivy, the navigator, has become a big fan of mine."

"What's new about that? She's been hanging around here every chance she gets. Just like a hundred other minions."

Bonnie shook her head. "I don't think so, Dezi. This is something different. Something personal." Bonnie swallowed, pensiveness deep in her voice, "I can always use another friend but she said something about wanting to have a baby together. I get this gender confusion with them all the time. It's hard to tell the males from the females in the first place and they don't seem to care since either sex can have a baby." She laughed ruefully. "I guess science really has come far on this planet." Bonnie raised an eyebrow. "Do you suppose she's serious?"

Dezi rolled his eyes. "I doubt it. It might be another form of worship. They're all crazy about us, or haven't you noticed?"

Bonnie yawned. "Yeah, I guess it's just their way. Maybe if I see Echo, I'll ask her about it." Turning to pick up Baby Peter, Bonnie asked, "Wasn't that something with Jose and Cobby tonight? I think Forbation and the rest of them have had just about enough from him."

Dezi moved to the bed to take the baby from her, swinging the now-awakened infant to his hip. "We gunna take him back to the nursery or let *them*?" The minions swung into attention as they realized it was time for the baby to go.

Bonnie gave them a smile and asked, "Do you mind if we all go together?"

Their mind auras danced happily in her brain, "Of course, Sister.

We would be honored." They scrambled from the end of the bed to accompany Dezi and Bonnie with the baby.

As they carried the baby down the hallway toward the nursery, Dezi commented, "I can't blame the poor guy, ya know."

"What poor guy?"

"Jose."

"Oh, yeah. I know what you mean. I feel bad for him too."

"If anyone was putting it to my wife, I'd have to kill 'em."

Bonnie looked askance. "It's not like any one of us are strangers, Dezi. Cobby's like a father to me and a brother to so many others. That makes it sticky. I'm surprised nothing like this had happened before. We've all been married for so long. I'm happy for Abby and Cobby. Even though it means someone gets hurt."

Dezi saw the damaged look coming back into her eyes. Changing the subject, he asked her, "So you've decided to work in the nursery with Chloe and Kenya? That's a lot of squalling babies, isn't it?"

Bonnie gave him a swift punch on the arm. "Yes, silly. What else would you have us mommas doing? Chloe is close to term and Kenya is gaga over babies now. Remember when she just wanted someone to cut the baby out of her stomach?" Bonnie rolled her eyes. "That seems so long ago . . ."

Dezi lifted Baby Peter from her arms, tucking the infant under one arm and slipping his other companionably through Bonnie's.

"Yes so much has happened . . . so long ago. I feel like I could write a book."

Bonnie turned and made a face at him. "You can leave me out of *that*."

Dezi gave her a bear hug, squeezing Peter between them. "I'm only kidding, you little dummy. Who would read it, after all?" They laughed together and happily made their way to the nursery, picking up more adoring minions along the way.

Jose clenched his teeth painfully as he continued to pace in his segregated bedroom on the other side of the Womb. Banished again to his punishment space, he had slept badly the night before. Now he was on Forbation's shit list again and would be unable to join the rest of the survivors for quite some time. He wondered what assignment he'd be forced to do today. *Probably cleaning up shit, I'll bet.* His bitter thoughts got the better of him.

He had thought he was making progress, especially when he tried to win favor with Netty by sucking up to Maya. The little girl had been walking around like the cat that ate the cream and resisting anyone that tried to play with her or get her to take off her fanny pack. With plenty of coaxing and one eye on Netty, he had managed to lasso the child and keep her attention long enough to recognize the odd bulge in her fanny pack. Unzipping it and nicking the small Beretta, he surreptitiously placed it in his own pocket as Netty's brow furrowed over Maya squirming in his arms.

Letting the child wriggle away, he took a seat at the end of the table. His eyes swept the empty chairs, calculating how to position himself so he would get a chance to talk to Abby. He just *had* to talk to her and make things better between them.

"Hello, Jose." Abby stood at the corner of the table looking down on him. She gave him a tentative smile. "I'm glad to see you back." Before he could answer, he saw an arm snake around her waist from behind her wing and lift her off her feet.

"Eek, you nut . . . let me down." Abby pealed with laughter as Cobby swept her off her feet and gave her a big kiss, not seeing Jose steaming in his chair. Abby rolled her eyes, trying to signal Jose's unexpected presence to Cobby.

Finally spotting Abby's soon-to-be ex-husband, Cobby set her down with a shrug and devilish grin, not missed by Jose.

"*Excuse me* . . . Abby and I were talking," said Jose, rising to his feet, his face a mask of tightness and controlled fury.

Fully understanding the boiling pot that was Jose, Abby stepped between the men. Attempting to be casual, she commented, "I'll have to get back to you, Jose." Glancing around the room, she saw most of the survivors had taken seats. Raising a hand, she waved to Chloe. "Save us a seat, hon. We'll be right there."

In desperation, Jose grabbed her arm as she began to walk away with Cobby. "No, Abby. *Now.*"

Before anyone could take a breath, Cobby shot to Abby's side to grip Jose's arm, his bloodless knuckles and flashing eyes attesting his anger. "I think she said . . . *some other time.*"

Jose jerked his arm free and in a blink had Cobby in a headlock. A furniture-splintering free-for-all ensued. When all the feathers had settled and screaming had stopped, Jose was left with a broken wing, entire handfuls of feathers yanked out of his limb. Cobby had blood seeping from an ear and Hud stood between the two men.

"If you two can't stow your testosterone, we'll need to make new arrangements. Now *cut the shit.*" His eyes bore into Jose. "Do you get my drift?"

Jose's face steamed. He took deep gulping breaths of air, trying to get himself under control.

Hud turned and continued. "You okay, Cobby?"

"Sure, I think we've had enough." Abby clung to his side, a cloth tossed from Dezi cleaning up the dribbling blood.

From the corner of his eye, Jose watched Cobby throw an arm around her shoulder and slip a kiss on her forehead. "Thanks, babe. I'll be alright."

That was the final straw for Jose. He lunged at Cobby, his lion-like tail snapping in the air. Cobby went down hard with Jose on top of him, Abby screaming. "Jose. No!"

Hud and Wil pulled Jose off Cobby but not before they all realized Cobby had hit his head on the hard floor; Jose's entire weight, wings and all, adding to the force. He was out cold.

Back in his solitary room, Jose scrunched his eyes closed and rubbed his forehead with both hands. He hadn't meant to hurt Cobby so badly. He just couldn't help himself. Who the hell was Cobby to be so possessive with Abby? She was *his!* He cringed when he remembered the faces of Kane and Kenya, Bonnie and Chloe. He hadn't been able to look Chloe in the eye after getting a peek at her tear-stained face. He knew the tears were for him while everyone's anger screamed for him to be banished. Before anyone could do anything, he turned on his heel and limped back to his hole-in-the-wall, but not before he got a clear look at Netty's cold expression and the disappointment in the lowering of Echo's golden furry head. *That means it's already all over the Womb, including Forbation.*

He flopped down on his bed, the stress of the day exhausting him as he watched the walls vibrate with movement, faintly expanding as the Womb breathed. It was becoming nauseating.

Feeling a lump in his bed, he reached under the mattress to feel the Beretta he had secreted. He didn't know what he planned to do with it but just having it there made him feel more like a man. With that thought in his head, he settled down and fell fast asleep. The long complex of niches and corridors cooled outside his meager room, silent as always, not even the soft flutter of minion wings to disturb the night.

# Chapter 12

Jose rose hurriedly, having overslept. He flapped his left wing gently; six inches of missing feathers and another hole further down made him look like something that would make even an earthly peacock hang its head in shame.

The minute he stepped outside his room, he knew something was different. No Forbation. The usual fawning minions fluttered above, taking a break from their usual duties to simper over their catching a glimpse of him. But instead of the Elder minion of the Womb waiting to castigate him and force him to grovel, there stood a miniature minion that stood only two feet tall, and she was rocking back and forth on her feet in excitement. Jose's mind accepted the minion's aura.

"Hello, Brother Jose. I am Sister Doodiet. Brother Forbation sent me to take you to your permanent work assignment. I will be in charge of you. We must hurry, hurry. The day is getting away from us."

"You're a female and Forbation put you in charge of me?"

The little minion's aura darkened. "You speak with disrespect, Brother. I am disappointed to begin our long relationship with such behavior. I will make a note of your disposition and hope that it will improve as we begin your duties." Doodiet took to the air. "Come, we are late as it is."

Doodiet joined the flock of minions overhead, each one's flight a syncopation of pathways in the air. Jose quickly shook out his wings to fly but realized walking would need to be his mode of travel until his plumage grew back. Further humiliated, he kept an eye out for Doodiet and followed her from below.

As he reached the main artery that ran through the Womb, he squinted his eyes against the Oolahan sun that streamed down to him from dizzying heights. When he looked up to locate Doodiet, he was overcome with vertigo and made faint by the layers and layers of minions that flew above him; golden wings fluttering, tails flying and crystal antlers flashing their black and red deadly emissions. It made for a stupendously blinding sight as the sunlight lit up the massive cathedral that was the ceiling.

Soon, his trek led him to an enormous metal plate sheltered in an alcove. A steady stream of minions collected at the base of the plate. Some pushed carts laden with parcels that were stacked with trays of weirdly fragrant organic material, rocks and a wild variety of mysterious objects for which Jose had no name; the silence was broken only by the wheels that carried their burdens.

Doodiet landed deftly before him, folding her delicate wings close to her body, not a strand of fur out of place. "We stop here. The plate will soon open. We must be in line."

As they joined the melee near the plate, Jose asked, "What's the big deal? Why is everyone waiting?"

Doodiet responded, her aura sharp and clear. "This will be your first lesson, Brother Jose. Behind this safety plate is the entrance to the most dangerous place on this planet. We are charged with the honor of caring for the wide variety of species as they are brought from the portals linking our worlds. We must study their behavior before actual work can be done on them."

Jose's mouth was agape. "What kind of work is done on them?"

"That is none of your concern, Brother. It will be up to us to monitor their behavior and make sure they are fed and kept comfortable and clean. When we have ascertained their level of danger, they will be put into rotation for study."

"Holy shit!"

Doodiet stood and stared blankly at Jose. Her aura finally sent him questioning fingers, which he ignored in his burgeoning anger.

"This is an effing zoo. And you're trying to tell me I'm just going to be a janitor for the inmates?"

Doodiet bristled. "You are sadly mistaken if you think you can take this assignment lightly, Brother Jose. If I were you, I would work very hard. Just like the rest of us. And if you are lucky, maybe Brother Forbation will forgive you for your demonstration of violence. I'll tell you a little secret, it is only due to the fact that you are a human, our very descendant, that has saved you from expulsion from our planet. Violence, when detected in any of our charges, is bred out of the species. That's part of why they are here. We will reintegrate the altered member back into the population of his planet and return with another member to alter. Over the multitude of generations, we have found the altered or non-violent members have an easier time of breeding, increasing the odds that someday in the far-off future, most violence will be vanquished from the planet."

"You must be kidding me."

"I assure you, Brother, I am not. Come, now." Doodiet moved forward with the crowd. An unexpected surge found all minions jockeying for position. "Hurry, Brother. The lock will not stay open for long. We have only a few moments to get through before it closes. There is no telling when it will open again."

"Well, that certainly sounds like a screwball system if ever I heard one."

Doodiet kept walking but her head twisted around to face Jose. "Please, Brother. There are necessary reasons for everything on Oolahan. Perhaps it would be best if you just listened until you learn your duties."

With those words, Jose crossed into his new working area he had dubbed "The Zoo".

It wasn't long before even the muttering stopped as Sister Doodiet escorted him around the most exemplary, mind-blowing and unending collection of never-before-seen life from all corners of the cosmos. He observed creatures of every size, shape, and color. Organic and inorganic. Most of the life forms were kept in a sealed room of safety glass with airlocks for ease in feeding and taking of cell samples.

"Sister Daisy was very useful when she was here," Doodiet's aura seemed to sigh in his mind. "She won't be back from her mission for weeks. I hope she has time to give us. We need her to speak to the new arrivals. It takes quite a while for them to settle down and get used to hearing voices in their heads. Some of them just . . . flip out and fail to adjust. When Daisy can communicate with them, they become a lot more cooperative."

"What's this over here?" Jose had sidled up to a glass room with a table that had a small glass-covered dish lying on it. Inside the dish sat a rock.

Doodiet peeked around the corner to investigate what had caught Jose's interest. "Oh, that. They are scumchi—minute life forms that thrive on minerals. They are from Chiox, a planet of nothing but rock, and some rudimentary plant life. The problem is the scumchi eat the rock. It's their excrement that provides an environment for the simple plant life to take hold. We are attempting to discover the evolutionary track for the scumchi. Will they consume the planet? How long will that take? Will it give the plant life time to evolve into something more substantial? Plants need minerals to survive too. Is it possible to introduce a new series of life forms to the plant? We have many species that we would like to migrate to other young fertile planets. Some of our scientists think the Chiox is ripe for colonization." Doodiet shrugged her slender furry shoulders. "It is a balancing act—critical and potentially deadly. We never know exactly *what* we will get when we do a colonization. Look at our failure with Homo sapiens. It has been a horror story. But most of the time we are successful. And remember, your planet was only the 6609th species intervention. So our numbers are actually pretty good."

Jose was speechless for a moment. "So let me get this right. I'm here to be a *zoo keeper?*"

Doodiet cocked her head, fur rising to stand on end. "Brother Jose, I detect a note of hostility. I am becoming uneasy. Brother Forbation will not be happy when I report to him that you are less then cooperative."

Doodiet's words sobered him abruptly. Kneeling in front of the diminutive minion he begged, "No, no. I'm very appreciative, Sister Doodiet. You misunderstood me." He grabbed the minion's leather hand, her suction cup fingers attaching themselves to him. "I beg you, Sister. Let me show you what a good job I can do." He looked around his surroundings and swallowed hard. "I'm grateful for this opportunity."

Apparently, Jose was convincing enough to sway Doodiet for she directed him to a hallway he had previously overlooked. Doodiet's aura darkened. "I need only show this location to you once." Jose's curiosity rose.

A metal door blocked the entrance to the hallway. Alongside the door was a small box made of metal and a stool underneath. Doodiet climbed the stool, inserted her hand in the box and extracted a round key. Climbing down, she tapped the key on the metal door near the floor. Stepping back, the door opened. Doodiet motioned him through with a warning. "Do not leave my side. Not even for a second." Jose's interest increased.

Together, they took a few steps into the hallway that was lined with the same glass chambers with airlocks attached. The only difference was the metal bars that surrounded each and every chamber in a tight web of a crisscrossing design. A few minions pushed carts laden with varieties of substance meant for the occupants. The minions wore head gear unlike anything he had seen before. A thin supple skin of clear insulation completely encased the minions and on their heads there was a small apparatus with tubes, covering their antlers and all.

"This is a restricted area. It contains some of the most lethal species known to minions. If a lethal species is not a guest here, it's because we haven't had time to get to it yet. I'm happy to report we have no Homo sapiens here . . . *yet.*"

"Just what do you mean by *yet,* Sister?"

Doodiet's aura brightened with sparkles and bright light. Jose watched her bend at the waist then straighten up. "Do you not know humor, my Brother? I was just trying some out on you. You did not laugh."

"Ya got me there, Sister Doodiet." Jose rolled his eyes. *What's next?* he asked himself. Turning back to his escort, he asked, "So this is a jail?"

Doodiet's aura remained silent then caressed his mind. "For some guests, yes. Their stay might be short-term, but only for a rare few. For the others . . . more like a prison; as it *should* be. Some of them are the last of their species. Come, we must suit up. If there is an unlikely accident, it will keep us free of contamination."

109

As Jose opened his mouth to speak, a resounding clatter, then crash was heard. Turning around, Jose saw a minion with a loaded cart had entered the hallway and bent to replace the key on the occupied side of the room. It appeared the minion had jarred the cart as he bent, sending the contents crashing to the ground. The minion stood, stress and anxiety obvious in the wild shaking of its arms. Doodiet waved her arms in return; the incident obviously a critical dilemma.

"I must give help, Brother Jose. Do not move. Our guests expect their sustenance on schedule. If not, some of them could die . . . or get quite riled." With hardly a glance for Jose, Doodiet rushed off to help salvage the mess.

Finally alone, Jose scanned the space. Other minions had rushed to help, creating a bottleneck around the toppled cart. Whistling to himself, Jose slowly wandered off. His impression of the gigantic space was that of a simple yet effective contamination lab; a hot lab. He wondered what sort of microbes were crawling around on the minion's "*guests*". As Jose wandered deeper into the restricted area, he was struck by an amazing fact. *The walls . . . what the heck is with the walls?*

Jose stood next to a wall and banged his hand on what appeared to be a hard substance. He placed his hand flat, feeling an uncomfortable coolness. But where was the Womb? With the exception of the survivors' quarters, all of the walls in the fortress were alive. He wondered about the difference in the security domain. Didn't the Womb want to keep an eye in here too? He tipped his head back to look up. No soaring ceilings with glorious light either. Continuing on, he came to a storage area of sorts. A line of empty spheres stood against the wall. Just like the sphere he'd seen the night they'd first set their eyes on Bonnie's friend IV, the navigator. *Bonnie calls her Ivey*, he remembered.

His attention returned to the spheres that took up most of the room at this end of the unusual space. Out of the corner of his eye, he spotted a lone glass chamber with its air duct surrounded by the metal bars to which he was already becoming accustomed. Looking around, he found he was alone. Eyeing up the glass prison, he noticed an empty cart to the side. *Feeding time over?* Sidling closer to the glass, he attempted to shake off a new creepy sensation. The deafening silence began to shriek at him.

He swallowed hard, his throat suddenly constricted and dry. Biting his lip and fastening his tail thoroughly to his chest, he crept closer. His heart began to hammer with the excitement of catching his first glimpse of a dangerous alien creature. Taking one last scan around to reassure himself he was safe from harm and discovery, he peeked through the glass, his vision somewhat restricted by the metal bars.

His heart stopped and he almost fainted as a slender shape with a massive head and a double row of hundreds of stiletto teeth from a maw dripping a rusty foam slapped up against the glass, almost as if it knew he would be there. And then it disappeared, having shown itself for less than a fraction of a second.

Jose blinked, his pulse racing, his skin wet with perspiration, clammy and cold. *What the fuck?* He noticed he had an almost irrational need to urinate. He hugged his damaged wings tightly to his body and considered disappearing back to his frugal room. Knowing it would be too hard to explain if he turned up missing from Doodiet's watchful eye, he hesitated. Breathing deeply, slowly, he attempted to calm himself down. Looking deeper into the glass, he observed clearly that the block was empty. *Nerves . . . just nerves*, he thought, completely overlooking the smears of rusty goo on the glass behind the bars.

Realizing the predicament he'd be in if he were discovered here, Jose casually high-tailed it back to the minions that were just dispersing, having completed the clean-up. Among the crowd, the diminutive Doodiet easily stood out. He felt her aura probing his mind.

"Where did you go, Brother Jose?"

Replying nonchalantly, Jose felt his face redden. "Nowhere, Sister. I just stepped back over there." He pointed to the storage area with the spheres and the frightening glass cage. *What's the point in lying? No harm done.*

Doodiet spoke. "Well . . . no harm done." Her aura spun slowly.

The minion shuffled over to stare up at him. Seconds ticked by as Jose's face began to redden again.

"I worry for your safety, Brother Jose. My Brother Forbation is correct when he says humans are unpredictable. Minions have relied on predictability and our insistence on non-violence for as long as life has existed. There is very little that confounds the Womb. Now that we are to live with Homo sapiens in concert, I pray to the Womb that all will be well. What do you think, Brother Jose?" She continued to stoically stand in front of him, her glowing golden eyes so much like his own.

"Ah . . . um . . . well yeah, I'm right there with you, Sister." Silence trickled by, his blood racing through his ears like a wind tunnel.

"Come . . . it is time I show you your duties."

Chastened and confused, Jose followed the gentle minion and gave her his undivided attention for the rest of the day.

Later that day, Jose lay exhausted in his bed, tossing and turning. His subconscious mind was restless even as he slept deeply. The first of the dreams came as he reached deep REM sleep.

A voice, light and lyrical with a faint cry. "Helppppp me. Pleaseeeeeeee." A quick flash of a slender blond woman, her hair full and rich, floating down past her knees as if birthing her from a cloud. A whisper. "Joseeee. I neeeed you."

The dream slipped away while Jose sank deeper into sleep, left only with an image of rusted foam splattered against a glass pane.

# Twenty Two Days AE (After Earth)

# Chapter 13

Dezi sat doodling on his papers in the kitchen. He'd just finished documenting the activities of the last few weeks. The documenting was so easy with his new recording device, all he needed to do was unscrew the metal tube, flip the metal lid, and press on the paper. Then he pictured the words he wanted to say. He could glance at the paper as he thought and the words would appear as if by magic. Echo had explained the device was actually a converter. Mental energy in was converted, and the interpreted words carved themselves out on his paper. So simple.

The crafty Forbation had been right. He understood now that Forbation had been worried for him. Cooking and running a kitchen would take the most devoted chef only so far.

As the only unattached male in their group, he needed an outlet. Hud didn't count as he was still grieving for Ginger Mae and Dezi felt sure he hadn't completely given up on the chance she might be found. So he'd decided to keep a diary with the papers Forbation had left for him. It had started as a simple exercise to document his feelings for Bonnie. Somehow, putting his feelings on paper allowed him to step back and accept the fact that there would never be any hope for him as long as the slightest spark remained that Peter might return.

From there it became a habit to record the highlights of their new life on Oolaha. The brawl between Jose and Cobby. The uncoupling/divorce ceremony Abby had participated in with Netty and Forbation. Dezi didn't want to be around when *that* little bomb was dropped on the rest of the group.

He had used up plenty of paper recording the excitement they all shared to hear that Daisy would soon be back from her first mission.

He had noticed many tears from the women around the table when Jose's cute little minion, Doodiet, came with the news. After a party to celebrate, Daisy would return to the restricted section where Jose worked. Dezi remembered Chloe's generous offer to pitch in with the festivities.

"Are you outa your mind, girl? You have a *baby* due in a couple a weeks." Kenya broke out in trills of laughter at the thought. "Let me tell you, chickey. Ain't no cakes needed enough to risk that amazing baby you been luggin' around for so long."

Abby chimed in, rushing to Chloe's defense. "I know how you feel, hon, we all miss her. But we can't afford to have you risk our little miracle baby. And in your condition, how much could you really accomplish?"

Chloe smiled at the good-natured ribbing and protested loudly. "I could crack eggs." The rest of the table groaned.

*Yeah,* thought Dezi. *Crack eggs. Just what I need, an enormous pregnant woman almost ready to give birth to the first human-alien minion in history and she wants to be cracking eggs in my kitchen.* Dezi shook his head as he put down the writing instrument.

Struck by a thought, he realized that two humans would be working in the fancy restricted area. It might warrant a lunchtime visit by him with their chow instead of sending Jose's lone fare with a minion.

Thinking of Jose, he wondered how he was making out. *I certainly understand why he hasn't rejoined the rest of us . . . now that Abby and Cobby have married. Wow, could it be that he doesn't know? The poor guy. Someone better clue him in.* Remembering the fists that flew a couple of weeks ago at dinner, Dezi decided it sure as hell wouldn't be him.

But if he could wangle a trip to the restricted area, he might see some sights to record in his diary. Opening it again, he made a note to interview Netty and Wil. It had been a long time since they'd shared a conversation. They usually flew in for meals, shouted greetings, gobbled some food and flew back to work. Dezi understood their experiments were important and they were learning much from the minion scientists, but if he didn't know better, he'd think he was slipping in the culinary department. Since when had anybody been able to resist his confections? Whatever they were working on, he knew it would make a great addition to his journal and he intended to pin them down.

Dezi yawned and stretched his arms high. He was sure he could make an effective case that would get him out of the kitchen when Daisy joined Jose in the restricted area. They both need to eat. He nodded his head, a satisfied smile spreading over his face. Perhaps he might even have a little adventure. *Yeah . . . maybe I could wangle a trip down there now. Just to get the lie of the land.*

He would start his own specialized delivery service. It would give him so much more to write in his journal as well. What possible harm could that bring?

# Twenty Three Days AE (After Earth)

# Chapter 14

Ginger Mae picked up the slops bucket she and Peter used for their waste and heaved it at the creature that had him in its grip. The odorous drippings coated them both, serving only to make the situation worse for Peter. Two other ungainly creatures grabbed her arms and subdued her, the accompanying buzzing of bees rising and falling in a frantic melody. She choked on the hot, acrid, burning smell that made its way inside her lungs every time she took a breath.

"*Noooooo.* You can't have him. *Please leave us alone,*" she begged fruitlessly. Her tears flowed unrestrained, futility wearing her down as the creature that had Peter in its grip slipped through the door. Forcing her to the ground, the other two creatures released her and quickly fled through the door as silently as they'd arrived.

Ginger Mae slapped her hand on the floor. "No, no, no, *no,*" she moaned. *When will this nightmare stop?*

The last few weeks had been such an improvement with Peter's company. He was a serious man but not without humor, and very intelligent. She admired that in him. Even though they couldn't recount and share memories from their pasts they were able to become very familiar with the attitudes, hopes and desires they both shared.

She closed her eyes and tried to block out the images of what their brutal captors might be doing to Peter.

A flush of blood stained Ginger Mae's cheeks as she recalled what had happened between her and Peter during recent weeks. She tried to recapture the thrill of their desperate lovemaking but found the lingering smell of the creatures interfered. She could feel the darkness in her psyche spread its tentacles, her newfound spirits a trophy for her inner demons that threatened to swamp the courage that Peter's presence afforded her.

She rolled onto her back and opened her eyes, the ceiling above a flat blank surface. Flexing her fingers and tightening them into a fist, she refused to accept the hopelessness of their situation. She could thank Peter for that. Her hunger for companionship had blossomed into something tender, something precious with Peter. And she knew he felt the same way. They had been brutally honest with one another. If they could ever find a way to get out of this infernal death trap, she knew she would like to spend as much time with Peter as possible. She felt an instinctive calm around him . . . a feeling of being where she belonged. Almost a feeling of comfort, of home . . .

She ran her hand slowly over the slight rise of her shivering abdomen. She could feel tenderness as she palpitated her still firm belly. *Could it be?* she wondered. Attempting to deduce the length of time they'd been held captive, and with the meager trove of medical wisdom she possessed, she gave up in frustration. Praying she was wrong, her eyes wandered around the cold bleak room. This was no place to birth a baby. She refused to contemplate what their captives would make of it.

Forcing the subject to the back of her mind, she flushed again, her good hand straying to the tender space between her legs where an aching and tingling forced her thoughts back to the wanton nature of their lovemaking.

He had filled her up and possessed her, worshiping her glorious breasts and urging her to new heights as their passion took on a wild and animal frenzy that seemed to last for hours. The following day, she found herself unable to keep her hands off him. Or her mouth . . . Her only desire was focused on pleasing him and making him want her more . . . she had to have more of him.

She blinked her eyes. *What the . . .?* She sat bolt upright and squinted her eyes to see what had caught her attention. Craning her neck, she twisted it at several angles to focus in on an imperfection she had spotted in the ceiling.

There appeared to be a straight line of demarcation that didn't quite blend. It looked to be a hair lower than the rest of the ceiling. Ginger Mae calculated the wall to be ten feet high before it met the ceiling. The imperfection was in the corner of the room, close to the wall. *Hmmm.* She examined it from all angles but failed to find a better viewpoint.

She would need Peter to lift her up. Her heart quickened. If he would let her stand on his shoulders, she could examine the discrepancy up close. Perhaps it masked a trap door. Or a vent . . . or the beginning of stairs . . . or the entrance to a time machine. Laughing, she fell to the floor with her giddiness getting the best of her. Who knew what it was? She smiled to herself and nodded. She would find out. This could be the break they were waiting for.

Without wanting to stop herself, she drifted back to thoughts of what she wanted to do to Peter. Over and over, again and again.

She couldn't remember any details of her former sex life and was surprised to find herself so . . . intense . . . so hungry. As her eyes fastened unwaveringly on the little miracle she had found in the ceiling, she squirmed, allowing her fingers to travel back down to that special spot as she basked in her happy glow and waited for Peter.

Ginger Mae slept long and deep, her satisfied stupor a drug to her system. She remained relaxed as she was assailed by her dream of hands reaching out to her, attempting to drag her away and the larger, heavier, capable hand on her shoulder. The meaning of the dream shifted around in her sleeping consciousness, even as she'd long ago dismissed it as a figment of her imagination; something wrought from the trauma of her captivity. She tossed in her sleep, murmured and curled up tighter on her pallet.

The persistent sound of buzzing bees woke her. Her eyes snapped open as her nose identified the hot burning trademark of her captors. *Peter!*

She scrambled to her feet and backed up against the farthest wall, pretending to be invisible. Her cry of alarm escaped as she took in Peter's horrifying condition. They had laid him out on his pallet, unconscious. The creatures with their alien demeanor cascading sparks, stood at the door watching her. She swallowed hard and turned back to Peter, a dressing clinging tightly to his shoulder joint where his arm used to hang. Gone. First his hand, now his entire arm. She held her hand to her mouth in terror. *Oh, my God. Someone, please come save us.*

A sound at the door drew her attention. Seconds passed as she stared, voiceless. Without warning, they pounced on her. She screamed at the top of her lungs, making her body go limp in an attempt to hinder her removal. Muscular arms wrapped around her body as she felt herself being lifted off the floor and moved toward the door. Cascading sparks touched her skin, landing like drops of cold ice. *God . . . no.*

"*Peter* . . . help me!" she screeched. Gathering all her might, she bucked in their arms, refusing to go quietly. "You dirty lousy pigs. Get your filthy pig hands off me!" she screamed, her eyes rolling back, wild and frantic, spittle frothing in the corners of her mouth.

At the door, she managed to free a leg, instantly pulling it up to her chest to let loose a jackhammer foot into the face of the nearest beast. Her ears hurt with the decibel of sound from the wounded creature. Before she could formulate another thought, she felt a prick at the back of her neck and the darkness came rushing to take her home.

Ginger Mae felt like she was drowning. She had no trouble breathing, but the arms and hands that waved at her from above exerted a puzzling pull on her. A dragging down. *Shouldn't it be up?* she wondered flippantly as if a drunken haze. The arms reached for her again as she began to flail. The sudden touch of a heavy hand calmed her. Her breath slowed . . . rhythmic and stable. Her consciousness swam from the depths of her dream.

Her eyes slowly opened. She focused blankly on the ceiling of her enclosure, her newly discovered faint possibility of escape staring her in the face without comprehension. No sign remained of the calming hand. A whisper penetrated her stupefied condition.

"Bonnie . . . Bonnie. Please . . . help me. Psst . . . *Bonnie.*" She heard a sob coming from the same direction. She reached up to rub her eyes awake and was shocked to feel pain. Letting her arms fall back to her pallet, she tried to lift them again; more pain. She carefully craned her neck back to locate Peter, observing him crawling toward her on the floor. *With one arm.*

Everything came flooding back to her. They *cut off* Peter's arm. She felt paralyzed with terror, her heart pummeling the inside of her chest. Peter's voice finally registered.

"My poor Bonnie." He was crying flat out, now. "What did they *do* to you? I'm so sorry, baby. The bastards. I'm gonna *kill* them."

As Peter broke down again, she struggled to sit up. Pain erupted all over her upper torso. Exhausted, she lay still, her heart threatening to explode, the sound of her rushing blood eclipsing her ability to hear. *What's wrong with me?*

"Peter? Can you help me?" Her words were met with more sobbing.

"Your beautiful breasts . . ."

"Peter, please stop crying. Can you maneuver over here and help me sit up?" A flash of annoyance overshadowed by a rush of sexual excitement overcame her. *Really? Now?*

She tried to tip her head back again to gauge his progress. Gratefully, he was on the move again. Inch by agonizing inch.

"That's it, Peter. Just a little more. Come on, baby."

As Peter reached her pallet, he loomed up over her, silent tears dripping from his face.

"How do you feel, Bonnie?"

His expression made her blood freeze. "I feel like a truck hit me. And I'm sure you don't feel much better. Can you help me sit up?"

He held out his one hand in protest. "No, babe. Just lie there. Let me get you some water. You look chalky."

She could hear Peter fumbling around with great difficulty.

"I can do it," he declared between gritted teeth, his breathing labored. He finally held the container of water to her lips, saying nothing as most of the water found its way down the sides of her face to dribble down her neck, soaking the pallet.

"Okay . . . okay," she choked. Peter set the container down, clumsily knocking it over, losing the rest of the water.

Ginger Mae took deep breaths, each word filled with pain, draining her strength. "What . . . *happened,* Peter? Your *arm* . . ."

120

She tried to reach for his hand. Feeling a constriction around her chest, her hands explored the area, finding bandages.

She began to hyperventilate. "No . . . *no.*" Shallow breaths came fast and hollow. Her brain refused to accept the shocking realization.

"*Nooooo.*" The room echoed with her anguish and terror as she realized the pert lovely breasts she'd been so proud of were no longer there.

# Twenty Four Days AE (After Earth)

# Chapter 15

Bonnie hugged Daisy as she entered the nursery.

"When did you get back? Have you seen Hud yet?" She could feel the lumpiness from the altered state around Daisy's neck. Her caftan didn't quite cover the bizarre changes to her body that her new skills necessitated. But that's what she'd wanted and everyone knew what a singularly focused young lady of a hundred and ten years or so Miss Daisy had been since she was a child.

"No, I haven't had a chance to find Hud yet." Daisy stepped back, her eyes searching Bonnie's face with the fragile, yet eternal hope of a heartbroken child.

"Mom and Peter?"

Bonnie lowered her eyes but she couldn't prevent a lone tear from brimming over onto her cheek, giving Daisy the news she didn't want to hear.

"Not yet, Daisy. I haven't been able to convince anyone to do anything about hunting for them. It's been weeks, now." She looked up, eyes flashing. "But I refuse to give up. Sooner or later, I'll find someone that can help me. I just *know* it." Bonnie noticed how subdued her tone sounded since so much time had passed. Was she, herself, beginning to doubt the viability of mounting a search?

Changing the sensitive subject, Bonnie dragged Daisy to a chair, shooing away the ever present and hovering minions. Bonnie shook off her perpetual malaise for Daisy.

"Enough of my problems. I want to hear everything about your first mission. Tell me everything."

Daisy clasped her hands together and stood to pirouette like the ten-year-old she resembled. "It was . . . I was . . . *oh my gosh* . . . how do I tell you? It was just literally out of this world." Her eyes gleamed almost as much as the minions.

"I was accompanied by a Kreyven and two minions who were transported with me inside one of the spheres. Apparently the propulsion device also maintains the atmosphere. We entered a portal after the Kreyven swallowed us. I couldn't see anything. But I knew I was safe. The Kreyven found the correct pathway and we landed on Tribith in no time at all."

Bonnie was in awe. "Tribith? Do you know where it is?"

"Not really," Daisy answered. "I do know it's in another solar system, with an atmosphere that is made up of an entirely different state of matter."

Bonnie wrinkled her brow. "What do you mean?"

Daisy explained. "Our atmosphere on Earth was made up of gases, just like here on Oolaha. Our molecules follow a set pattern of physics. Protons and neutrons attach to a molecule in different sequences to create a substance such as water. Two hydrogen atoms and one oxygen. But that's not what happens on Tribith. I had a hard time even seeing the Tribithians. They were just forms that flashed into view, erratically. Their molecular make-up was unstable to us which made it difficult for them to stay in view. But as I learned from them, it was us that were difficult to see. We were just empty space to them. A blank, empty space created by stable atoms. That actually made us easy to identify because they don't have empty space on Tribith." Daisy observed Bonnie's eyes glaze over. She clapped her hands, making Bonnie jump.

"Enough. I think it's time you let me fuss over the babies—if we can pry them away from their fan club."

They both turned to watch the minions that crowded the nursery fussing over the babies. Every minion that could get a finger in edgewise was stroking an infant, and the babies gloried in the attention.

Bonnie and Daisy rose happily, completely absorbed in the adoration of Peter and the other infants, just as offspring are worshipped and admired the universe over.

"Can I?" asked Daisy. She looked up at Bonnie for permission. Bonnie picked up her son, anxious minions hanging on until the last second. She placed Peter in the arms of her friend, seeing the look of longing on the face of a young woman that clearly knew she may never experience the singular joy of having a child of her own.

After Daisy left to find Hud, Bonnie sat to rock Peter. The room still fluttered with minions but Bonnie was so used to them by now that she just ignored their attentions.

Out of the corner of her eye, she caught a glimpse of a streak of fire. In a blink, Ivey stood in front of her, the fire butterfly that lived on her crystal antlers sending streaks of firelight up toward the ceiling.

"Hello, my Sister. I have been missing you."

Bonnie gave a gentle tightening of her lips, her energy drained from another stressful day.

"Do you not feel well, Sister?"

Bonnie shook her head. "Just a little blue, Ivey."

The minion gave Bonnie a thorough inspection. "I do not see the blue, Sister. Perhaps you are having trouble with your eyes?"

Bonnie laughed. "I sure am happy to see you back, Ivey. No one cheers me up like you do."

Ivey's aura brightened as she preened at the compliment. "You cheer me up too, Sister. I thought only of you on my last mission. Are you ready to marry me yet?"

Bonnie laughed out loud. "You never give up, do you, Ivey?"

Thinking she'd done something to make Bonnie agree, Ivey hopped from foot to foot and waved her arms. Her aura spiked in colors and busts of light. "You will not be sorry, Sister. We will be very happy together. Oh and with the baby too." She patted Peter's blanket. "I can't wait to share the news." She reached up on her toes and gave Bonnie a hug. "But first I must give you a surprise to show how much I love you." Without further comment, she took to the air and flew off. Bonnie was left speechless, her mouth hanging open. *Uh oh . . . I think it's time to speak to Netty and Forbation. What in the world have I done?*

Jose hurriedly dumped his waste collection into the tube that would carry it to be sorted into various useful components, even fertilizer that would be sent to Kane to distribute to the crops in his care. Nothing went to waste on Oolaha. He wouldn't be surprised if some of the waste wasn't recycled into the pillow on which he lay his head every night. He grinned to himself. Yes, the pillow that transported him into the best sleep he'd ever had. Not to mention the best dreams. He grinned again with the salacious memories then blushed as he remembered how Leeja had taken him into her lithe arms last night as he dreamed.

Jose straightened, adjusting the contamination suit that pinched him under the arms and in the crotch. *I think I need to have an anatomy lesson with the minions that make these suits.* He discreetly tugged at the wedgie in his rear.

Glancing around, he saw minions attending to the needs of those who were held captive. He'd seen many come and go in the spheres since he began working here. But not Leeja. In the beginning, he'd been cautioned to stay away from her enclosure and he had, for she resided in the one off-limits enclosure that Doodiet had said was the most dangerous, the one tucked away past the storage area. Jose had honestly tried to give his insipid responsibilities the earnest attention everyone demanded. But he had become a captive of his dreams. Of the call of Leeja.

He had decided to find a way to see her. It hadn't taken long. Once he convinced the minions he worked with that he was trustworthy, they left him to his own devices. Doodiet came to check on him once or twice a week. She'd even informed him he was welcome to return to his old bedroom with the rest of the survivors.

Jose puffed up his chest. *Oh, no . . . never.* Not with his Leeja here. He needed to be as close to her as possible. He might not be able to be with her physically now and the dreams would need to suffice, but every once in a while, he was able to see her in the flesh.

When he remembered the first time, his heart beat wildly and his blood pounded in his ears. He'd been on his way to collect the waste from her enclosure, which was on the other side of the room from where it would normally be found. A mild inconvenience and disappointing since it forced him to avoid passing the front of Leeja's glass block. As he navigated the waste tubes, he made up his mind. If no one was about, he would walk up to the glass and take a bold peek.

Heading back, he heard the fluttering of minions overhead. Obviously hellbent on their own destinations, they paid no attention to him. Swiftly scanning the floor around him, he realized he was alone. It was now or never.

He hurriedly made for the front of the glass box. Peering in, he noticed a lithe figure swaying. He swiped his arm across the glass to clear the grime. Moving forward again, he was startled by the face that plastered itself to the glass. It was Leeja. *Holy shit*, he thought. *She's human.* Jose's mind was a blank as he feasted his eyes on the lovely face and scads of thick, wavy blond hair that fell in swathes to cover most of her body, including her feet. He caught faint glimpses of impudent breasts as they peeked through the mass of hair that draped them.

*They lied. Doodiet lied to me. Could I have misunderstood?* Jose pondered. *Should I mention this to Netty and Wil? Did they know? Another human survivor is huge news.* Jose watched as she opened her mouth and smiled at him, then she lifted a slender hand with extraordinarily long fingers, and waved tentatively. Falling under her spell, he scanned the area, then waved back. He could see she was moving her lips. He shrugged and pointed to his ears, shaking his head. She continued to move her lips again, frustration waltzing over her face. He held up his hands and shrugged his shoulders. She dropped her hands as a blank expression bloomed on her face. To his consternation, tears dripped from her eyes as she mouthed a lone two words.

*Help me.*

Jose rocked back on his heels. There was no missing the message. He banged against the thick safety glass, but no sound was forthcoming. Having gotten her attention anyway, he watched as she held her hands together as if in prayer and placed them under the side of her face as if to sleep. She then pointed to him then to herself, raising an eyebrow. *She wants to know if I'll sleep with her.* She then pointed to her mouth and motioned to him and back to herself. *Oh . . . she wants to talk when I go to bed.*

That's when Jose realized the erotic woman in his dreams was none other than Leeja. She had been communicating with him. *How the heck did she learn to do that? And why is she here in this restricted area? Something's fishy.* Knowing anything was possible on Oolaha, Jose accepted her wondrous talent and began to live for his nocturnal dreams.

For that was where they made love; slow and tender, rising to the frenzy of passion that always concluded as he awoke the next morning. It would end with him promising to obtain her release. Exactly how to achieve this continued to elude him. For if he were to release her without permission, they would be in major trouble and definitely punished. Who knew what Forbation might do to them?

He knew the airlocks were never locked. The only way in was from the outside, for the handles were only *on* the outside. Yet, working in the restricted area was his last chance to be accepted back into his group of survivors. Perhaps, if he could make himself indispensable, a fearless and committed worker, maybe he could go to Forbation to ask this favor.

Just imagine what a hero he would be if he could bring another human into their group. He pushed the nagging question of why she was here to begin with to the back of his mind.

But it would take time. He must first do the hard work. In the meantime, he would have plenty of opportunity to get to know Leeja better. If he could just figure out how they could talk through the glass.

Jose's thoughts returned to the present. He longed to show up at Daisy's party tonight with Leeja on his arm. But deep in his heart he knew something must be wrong if Leeja was kept in the glass enclosure.

*But maybe they're just keeping her here to study her communication powers. Maybe they want to see if she inherited them from them. We are descended from them, after all.*

A ruckus sounded from the airlock entrance. Jose turned to see Daisy enter with Hud and Doodiet who began to show them around. He hurried over before Doodiet spotted where he was.

Wrapping his arms around Daisy, he lifted her off her feet.

"I am so happy to see you back, kiddo."

Daisy shrieked with laughter. Jose set her back down to watch Doodiet who was clapping her hands together and hopping from foot to foot, enjoying the excitement of their antics.

"I'm happy to be back too, Jose." She smoothed down her smock and readjusted it over the layers of cartilage at her neck. Doodiet's eyes gleamed, sending flashes of gold in their direction followed by her aura.

"I want to be a kiddo, too." She held her hands up to Jose to be lifted in the air as he had done to Daisy.

Jose stepped back. "Kiddo is just an expression, Doodiet. It's slang for kid." Doodiet's arms continued to reach out, her fingers wiggling in anticipation. Sighing, Jose reached down and gave the tiny minion a swing while her aura screeched in his mind. Setting her down, she wobbled then caught her balance.

"That was wonderful. Perhaps we can enjoy that again later."

Daisy covered her mouth with her hands, suppressing a laugh. "Maybe at my party tonight, Doodiet. You will be coming, won't you?"

"Oh yes. *Many* of us will be coming. Who would not come? Sister Daisy is our most remarkable descendant. We will celebrate her safe return."

Hud slipped his arm around Daisy's waist. "This is all I have left of my family. I'm sure happy to have her home for a while."

Hud panned the huge area, blinking at the occupied enclosures. "So this is where you and Jose will be working? With your talent, I can't imagine you'll be scooping poop along with him." Hud turned to Jose whose face showed a slow burn climbing from his neck. "I didn't mean how that sounded, Jose, sorry."

Daisy jumped in to distract. "No, I'll be used for communication. Some of the specimens here can only communicate in other ways . . . other than thoughts."

Jose cocked an eyebrow. "Specimens? Isn't that a little *harsh?"* Before anyone could answer him, the sound of the main airlock rang followed by a human voice. They all turned to watch Dezi emerge with a basket in his hand.

"Hey, dudes," he hailed. "Glad to see you all together. I come bearing gifts."

"How did *you* get in here, Dezi?" Jose bristled.

The cocky chef brandished a grin. "Well, if you aren't hungry, Jose, I can just pass your lunch on to Daisy." He bent to give her a kiss on the cheek. "Welcome back, sweetie. We have a lot planned for you tonight. Nothing like a beautiful doll like you to brighten up the place."

Jose reached into Dezi's basket to pull out his lunch. Wordlessly, he lifted a hand to the small crowd and disappeared deep into the storage area to eat his lunch. He sat at a metal table where he still had a vantage point of the airlock, Hud's words still stinging.

Suddenly, another minion appeared . . . a special one, followed by traces of flames from the fire butterfly embedded in her antler.

The commotion of Ivey's appearance increased as Daisy looked crestfallen and Dezi gesticulated wildly. Hud held up a silencing hand, hugged Daisy, and watched her leave with the minion sporting the butterfly. Dezi continued to stomp his feet and make a fuss.

Wondering what had just happened, Jose finished his lunch with a hunk of braebread to spare. One of Dezi's wonderful delicacies. It tasted better and better each time he tried it with its delicate texture and otherworldly flavors.

Dismissing the antics going on at the airlock entrance, Jose had a daring idea, his new bravado bolstered by his old resentments, which had flowered anew since Hud's put-down. Sinking further into the dimness of the storage area, he furtively made his way back to Leeja's enclosure. He eyed her airlock as he fingered his head apparatus and weighed the braebread in his hands.

*Why the hell not?* Promising himself he'd be quick, he turned the handle to his side of the airlock and stepped through the threshold. The memory of Leeja's lovemaking colored his emotions. Spurning caution, he planned to leave Dezi's delicacy for his new love. Inside the airlock, he set the braebread on the raised platform she was fed from. He reached out to place his hand flat on the door that separated him from her loveliness. All he had to do was press a button to let her in.

His heart thumped with excitement, lust and resentment. He took a deep breath and got himself under control while fighting with the unexpected image of Cobby and Abby making love. He clenched his fist tightly, his tail slapping against his thigh, his wings rustling with tension. He backed toward the outside door, resisting the impulse to let Leeja out for just a minute. As he lifted his foot to step outside, he pressed the button to open her door and prepare to close his door. He sniffed a sudden stench of rotted flesh and winced from a flash of pain. His only thought was of Leeja's safety as he fell to the ground, warmth from the iridescent blood that poured from the deep laceration across his face luring him toward the dark and blessed unconsciousness that blanketed him.

# Twenty Six Days AE (After Earth)

# Chapter 16

Ginger Mae lay listlessly on her filthy pallet in the cold empty room. Her eyes remained unfocused as she stared at the ceiling in wonder, the protruding lip in the corner of the ceiling obvious. Her mind played the same question over and over, a needle stuck on an old forty-five from the 1950s.

*Something about that ceiling . . .*

"Bonnie, I'm scared." The emaciated man that lay next to her pawed ineffectually at her arm. *What was his name again?* she wondered.

*Something about that ceiling . . .* Her claw-like hand roamed over her protruding abdomen, her pregnancy one of the few things her mind retained. That and the overriding fear that the monster would try to take her baby.

She brought her hand up to her mouth to cough, spewing a thin stomach gruel. She clutched her threadbare blanket for warmth, her body spasming with shivers. No matter how much she ate, her weight was dropping fast.

"Bonnie, I'm gunna be sick again."

The sound of retching echoed in the barren room. Acrid smells reached her nostrils, forcing her to heave the remaining gruel from her stomach. It wasn't the first time. Her hand wiped the residue of vomit from her chin. She rolled flat on her back exhausted, trying to alleviate the pain from her chest surgery, now just a dullness that spoke of her lost breasts.

"Bon . . . you okay? Come *on* . . . talk to me. We gotta get out of here, Bon. I don't think I'm gunna make it if we don't leave soon." He coughed; a deep phlegmy rattle that spoke of his infected chest. *Probably pneumonia.* She wondered how she might know that then her mind wandered off as if untethered to a single thought. Searching . . . searching . . .

She tried to distract herself by saying the baby's name over and over. A mantra of love: *Daisy . . . Daisy . . . Daisy chain . . .*

She knew she already loved the baby and prayed it was a girl. She was aware her thoughts were easily diverted these days. Again, she evaluated the ceiling, breathing deeply and sucking in a squalid whiff of unwashed bodies.

*The ceiling . . . yes.* Finally she was gifted with a moment of clarity. *Our escape.*

*"Get up, get up."*

She sat up slowly and tugged on the arm of her companion.

"Easy, Bonnie . . . easy." The man allowed himself to be coaxed to his feet where he stood weaving and off balance. His only arm acted as a rudder.

They gave each other stoic assessments. Two people close to death, maimed, bald, and starving . . . yet a tiny spark of naked purpose peeked through their dull and filmy eyes.

"We're *survivors,* Peter." His name tripped off her lips, her mind beginning to focus. "We *have* to do this."

Peter weaved on his heels.

"Do *what*, Bonnie?"

She pointed to the miracle in the ceiling . . . a chance of escape sent by God himself; if they could only prove themselves.

"I don't know. It looks awful high. And I don't think I can hold you long enough." He held up his lone arm.

"We need to *try,* Peter. For the baby." She began to pull at their pallets as she spoke, piling them on top of one another.

Peter moved to help. "No. Save your strength." He held out his arm to stop her, pulling her toward him so he could touch her belly; a small smile tugged at his lips, the effort difficult.

"Yeah, the baby."

He focused on her eyes. "Don't you think the baby grew fast? You look like you've been pregnant for a long time. Months . . . maybe four or five. But I know we haven't been here that long, have we? Are you worried, Bonnie?"

She rested her head on his shoulder, fighting not to collapse and throw in the towel. Her head rocked back and forth. "No . . . no . . . no. You don't know how long we've been here. We just need to focus on getting out of this hellhole."

She straightened up and took his head between her hands. "You love me?"

Peter nodded and held her tight.

"You love the baby?" Again he nodded.

"Then you *must* concentrate. It's our only hope."

Together they stood in the cool, unyielding room; two scrawny souls that should have died already under the mystifying hands of an alien species.

She glanced up at the ceiling again. Not good odds. But Ginger Mae didn't know about odds. She only knew survival.

She refolded the pallets, increasing their height by a probable eight inches. She moved Peter into position and assessed his condition. "Can you get on your knees, Peter?"

He complied, steading himself with his one arm.

"I'm going to straddle your shoulders and then I want you to stand."

"Bonnie, I don't think . . ."

"*Don't* think, just do what I tell you to do. We'll be *fine.*" She rolled her eyes and said a prayer.

Stepping up onto the pallets, she slipped a skinny leg around Peter's grimy neck. Carefully, she swung the next one around and held tightly to his head; her hands gripping his greasy forehead. She hunkered down tightly with her bulging abdomen pressed hard into his neck.

"Now, Peter . . . try to stand. Stay as balanced as you can."

Peter slid one knee back to brace himself, raised the other leg and rested; half up and half down.

"So far so good," he breathed heavily. "You feel very light. You okay up there?"

"Yes," she said impatiently. "Let's try your other leg. This is the hard one."

Peter's lone arm gripped her legs tighter and he slid his knee back toward his standing leg for leverage. Tipping Ginger Mae forward, he struggled to rise.

"You *made* it. Good going, Peter. Now walk toward the corner of the room. No . . . the corner."

Peter began to stagger under her weight as he took a few steps.

"Don't *drop* me, Peter. Come *on* . . . you can *do* this."

Red in the face and snorting, Peter made his way to the corner where Ginger Mae braced herself on the walls. She peered up.

"Oh no." Wiggling her fingers she raised her arms to the ceiling. A good foot short.

"I'm going to need to stand on your shoulders, Peter. It's the only way. We're a foot short. Maybe if I can get one foot up on your shoulder it'll be enough for me to reach. Just give me a minute."

She studied the lip in the ceiling. She could now see it was part of a hatch. She prayed it worked on a downward hinge. She would have trouble with it if she needed to lift upward.

"Okay. You still with me, Peter? I'm going to start . . . so please brace yourself and hold tight to my left leg." She could feel Peter shift his arm, freeing her right leg for lifting.

"Go ahead, Bonnie. You better hurry. I don't know how much longer I can hold you."

Ginger Mae rested her elbow on Peter's head, gripping him hard around the neck and shoved off, bringing her foot up to his shoulder. Reaching up she found she could almost touch the lip.

"I'm going to need to throw myself up so hold on. *Do not drop me.*"

"*Hurry up.*"

She could feel Peter begin to wobble. Gathering all her strength, Peter's head now digging into her abdomen, she tried to lever herself up, hoping to straighten her leg and gain the height she need to grip the lip and yank down.

"*I can't hold you, Bonnie!*" Peter screamed.

"Yes, you *can*, you son of a *bitch.*" She bit her lips and strained. Peter's fingers were like needles in her other leg.

"For *Christ's sake*, Peter. Stop digging into my *leg*." Suddenly, she knew. They were going down.

"*Ahhhhh.*"

"*Peterrrr.*"

Her head landed on the pallets, her leg hit the hard floor with a crunch. Looking over at Peter, she noticed he hadn't done as well; his face was flat on the floor and blood pooled around his forehead.

"Ugh . . . Peter . . . *Peter* . . . you okay?" She couldn't help herself from crying. All of her strength was drained, she couldn't move her leg, and her lover might be dead. The tears flowed heavily. She turned her head to the ceiling. Worst of all . . . they would never get out of here. Her hopes dashed, she dissolved into a hopeless morass of anguish.

So lost in her own misery, she failed to hear the door open. The burnt odor that portended terror finally hit her nose. Immediately, her heart stopped, terror sweats drenched her and she stiffened. Lifting her face from the floor, she couldn't believe her squinting eyes.

A young child in prodigious robes stood in the doorway. Her mouth was open but her lips failed to move as the monsters' bee buzzing tripped off her lips in lilting form. Alongside her stood a glowing animal with gleaming antlers and a bulbous lion-like tail. They were both dressed in a wrinkled bubble that followed the curvature of their forms, sealing them in. Small identical breathing devices hung from their backs and extended into their wraps. But most incongruous was the creature's wings that wafted in the cold and the most amazing butterfly that sat on the glass antlers trailing sparks and flames behind them.

In a complete panic, Ginger Mae screamed in terror and pain as she dragged her skeletal frame and broken leg to the far side of the room. She lay exhausted and mumbling to herself, her arms clasped around her abdomen to protect the baby.

The buzzing child let loose a tirade of buzzes, harsh and demanding, unimpeded by the wrap that insulated them. The stink of the aliens' burnt odor increased as several entered and approached Peter.

Ginger Mae clasped her hands to her mouth, anxious to suppress a moan. Tears depleted her as she prepared for Peter's death.

"You will be safe now, Mother."

Ginger Mae looked up in horror as the child approached her. Overtaken with terror, her shock complete, Ginger Mae was now dumb to her surroundings. The child waved the creatures forward.

Mutual buzzing commenced, cold sparks falling from the beasts as they lifted Ginger Mae in her catatonic state and took her through the door after Peter.

Outside the safety of her refuge, Ginger Mae's unseeing eyes glazed over the sight of Peter being restrained on a plank and carried inside a clear sphere where the golden creature with the butterfly directed the beasts to lock him into position.

A sudden flicker of light bloomed in her eyes as they rested on the mammoth creature that waited behind the sphere. It reared its eyeless head; gelatinous flesh with striating flashes of light that soared over the arcane proceedings.

Ginger Mae felt herself carried toward the sphere where she was strapped alongside Peter. The figures of the child and the golden creature wavered in and out of her limited vision.

From her supine position, she watched as the monstrous creature from above opened its dark maw and thrust forward to devour the sphere and the lives inside, thrusting them into darkness. Oddly, she was comforted.

Ginger Mae let her eyelids droop closed as her mind searched deeply for an answer . . . a clue . . . a reason to hold on. As her consciousness began to take leave, she murmured "Daisy," and stroked her abdomen, never realizing the strange child had slipped her tender hand into Ginger Mae's.

"I'm here, Mom. Time to come home."

# Twenty Seven Days AE (After Earth)

# Chapter 17

Kenya, Chloe and Echo sauntered along the corridor that let to Jose's lonely quarters, Caesar padding softly behind. Their heels clicked in the silence, echoing off the breathing walls of the hallway.

Chloe rubbed her abdomen, feeling a stomachache in the making. "I shouldn't have stuffed myself tonight."

Kenya pranced ahead a few steps, twirling and high stepping with glee. "You don't get to look *this* gorgeous belting down Dezi's goodies, chickey."

"Oh, *you*. That's not fair. Did I pick on *you* when you were pregnant? Besides . . . I felt bad for Dezi, all his hard work and yummy food going to waste." She licked her lips as she admired the food basket carried by Echo. "I couldn't let that happen. I still don't see why Daisy had to go back out on a mission so fast. Give the girl a break."

Echo's aura interrupted, "What is it that you want Sister Daisy to break, Sister Chloe? I promise I will see that she does the first thing after she returns."

Chloe laughed and tickled Echo on the back where her wings met. A squirming Echo suddenly stopped dead in her tracks. The golden minion tipped her head back and looked straight up. Chloe and Kenya followed her gaze. In a hushed voice, Chloe asked, "Oh, my heavens. Where is everyone?"

They stared at the empty space above their heads. Not a minion in sight. The Womb's walls pulsed alone, fading sunlight casting beams into the void. Chloe and Kenya turned back to Echo, quizzical expressions looking for guidance.

Echo remained motionless as seconds passed. She slowly raised her head, a tense expression overlaid with fury. Her aura was black and riotous. "There is great danger . . . much death. We must hide."

Kenya and Chloe reached for each other, Chloe cupping her abdomen to support the baby.

Echo moved to Chloe. "I can only save one. Quick, kneel down." Echo spread her wings. "I will come back for you, Sister Kenya. I must save Brother Scotty's baby."

"But we're almost at Jose's quarters," cried Kenya. She turned to hear Caesar hiss, his body in a full crouch.

Echo's aura faded. "We must *run.*" The group jumped and ran down the corridor. They turned the corner and Jose's doorway appeared. Darting inside, they looked for cover.

Kenya scrambled to the bed and threw herself on the floor. "Come on, everyone. Get under the bed." She slapped the floor. "Caesar . . . come." The big tiger crawled under the bed as Echo and Chloe got on the floor, Chloe's breath coming in rough heaves.

"I can't do it. I'll never fit. Go Echo. Kenya, grab Echo. I'll hide behind the bed." Chloe raised herself off the floor, her cumbersome figure slowing her down.

Echo's aura hit them hard. "No, *let me go,* Sister Kenya. I can save us. I need to get to the wall. Let me go."

Chloe suddenly sniffed, a miasma of spoiled meat slapping her in the face. Her heart beating painfully, she rushed to the side of the bed that hugged the Womb's wall. Squeezing into the tight space, she shimmied down to the floor, sliding her hands under the mattress to encounter something hard and metal. Gulping air, she tried to slow her tripping heart and ragged breath.

She heard Kenya mumbling under the bed. "Shhh . . . something's coming, I can smell something bad."

The rustling under the bed stopped as everyone tried to contain their terror. Chloe could feel Echo probing her mind, exerting a calming influence. "Do *not* move, Sister Chloe."

The odor of spoiled meat filled the room. A slithering sound reached their ears, turning their blood to ice. Chloe slowly raised her head to peek. Unable to control herself, she screamed.

Standing at the doorway, an eight-foot aberration lurked. Its massive head supported a molten and bubbling mass with slits for eyes that contained a malevolent and psychotic glare. But it was the mouth that caught her attention, rows and rows of slashing teeth that dripped with a thick rusty substance. Its slab of a tongue lolled to the side to swipe at the rusty goo. Then it vanished.

As the strains of Chloe's scream faded, she blinked. Suddenly, standing before her was Scotty; an eight-foot Scotty with slender olive plant-like arms that reached out for her. She reached across the bed as he held out the strange arms for her. She blinked again and he disappeared,

"Owww." One of the arms of the creature had slashed across her hand, opening the skin on her palm. Blood ran down onto Jose's bedcovers as the creature reappeared, its tongue lolling from the side of its mouth to slobber its rusty saliva down its neck. Its mouth flexed in glee. And in an instant, it vanished again.

"Please, Sister. Stand back." Echo crawled out from under the bed, her fire butterfly closed and sparkless. She stood and faced the area where the creature had vanished. From the empty space came an angry roar, livid at Echo's defiance. It reappeared and made ready to pounce.

"Stop, Echo. It has Scotty."

There before them both appeared the apparition of Chloe's dead love and Echo's best buddy.

"No, Sister. It is the power of the creature. Trust in me. I will save us." As Echo spoke, her crystal antlers split, dropping an implant in her hand. The red and black missile made for the creature, landing on its nose. It raised its razor-edged, plant-like arms to remove the offense, slicing its nose in the process. In a wink the implant snaked up the creature's nostril. The monster snorted, sending rusty drops flying, then fell over with a crash.

"Kenya . . . let's go . . . let's go." Chloe ripped Jose's bed sheet and wrapped a piece around her hand to stem the blood. Caesar pulled himself out and approached the monster, sniffing and chuffing with suspicion. Echo's aura hit them all.

"We must go. I don't know how long it will be out or how malleable it will be upon waking." She turned to Chloe and watched her tears. "*Please*, Sister. We must go."

Kenya stepped around the creature. "You don't need to tell me twice. *Come on,* Chloe."

Chloe hesitated. "I guess that wasn't Scotty I saw?"

Echo took her hand and yanked her out from behind the bed. In her other hand, behind Chloe's back, was the Beretta Jose had hidden under his mattress. She slipped it thoughtlessly into her skirt. "Echo, please tell me. If there's a chance . . ."

"No Sister. That was just a manifestation of the creature's evil powers. We are not sure what else it can do. But it is a death machine and it has been unleashed. We must get to safety. *Now.*"

The foursome left Jose's room, Chloe breathing heavily and waddling with difficulty, her lost blood soaking the makeshift bandage through.

"I'm not going to make it, Kenya."

"Come on, chickey." Kenya grabbed Chloe's good arm and placed it over her neck to support Chloe's weight.

Echo held up her hand. "I have sent for help, my Sisters."

From behind them, they heard snorting. *The creature.*

Echo stepped to the Womb's wall and inserted her arm. The wall separated and Echo stepped back to admit a colorful house Kreyven. Looking over their shoulders, they fled toward the Kreyven; it scooped them up into its maw amid female screams and wild, angry hissing. The Kreyven slipped back into the Womb's wall and disappeared just as the creature stepped from Jose's doorway waving its razor appendages, the smell of ripe carrion wafting before it.

As soon as the Kreyven expelled their sphere from its protection, Daisy, Ivey and the accompanying minions clapped and breathed a sigh of relief. One never knew for sure if the return trip would happen or not. So many dangers lurked on alien planets.

Daisy strolled from the sphere and looked around in puzzlement. She turned to watch her mother and Peter wake to vomit in the smaller sphere in which they were being floated.

Ivey cast a happy aura. "We must get them to the Healer. We cannot have them die on us now. I must present a healthy specimen to Sister Bonnie."

Daisy felt a prickle of unease. "Ivey, where is everyone?" She spread her hands to encompass the air space that should be teeming with minions ready to help, and the hundreds that came just to satisfy their curiosity. News of two new humans should have brought thousands. She turned back to Ivey who was now doubled over, as if in pain. Glancing past the navigator, she could see the minions with her mother were in distress. *"What?"* Daisy reeled with terror as Ivey's aura slammed into her.

"Danger . . . *death*. Oh no . . ." She signaled the sphere. "Come, Sister. We must protect ourselves. We must get to the Healer and seal it up."

They headed for the minion city on a run, the sphere floating with Ivey directing it from the top, the other minions fluttering alongside to monitor Ginger Mae and Peter who were now out cold. A trumpet of elephants could be heard in the distance.

Daisy failed to see a sign of life anywhere. All surrounding portals were unattended and empty, even though the nighttime was always busy with comings and goings.

The Womb loomed larger. She caught her breath as she realized the walls had darkened, leeched of all color. As they approached, she could see the Womb flexing horribly. Terror ran through her veins like a thief climbing prison walls.

*"Oh my God, Ivey.* What's going on?"

Ivey stood tall on the top of the sphere, her attention focused on the city. "We are not going to make it." Ivey's aura faded.

Daisy's head whipped around. "What do you mean, we're not going to make it? We're almost there."

"No, the Womb will protect the planet. It will close up so any danger does not escape."

Daisy ran faster, her ears refusing to believe. "But Mom . . . Peter . . . they can't wait. They need medical care *now*, Ivey."

"I am sorry, Sister. We have done all we can. Just hurry."

They didn't have far to go now; maybe the length of a football field. Incongruously, she remembered the stories Scotty and Kane used to tell her about the great and famous New York Jets from bygone years. If she could just move faster, like one of their legendary football players. She couldn't lose her mother. Not now . . . not ever. Daisy realized how panicked she was over the idea her mother might die. Her heart yearned for her mother's touch, her mother's arms. So close . . . Her despair made her stumble and down she went.

Ivey hesitated, slowing her speed. Daisy lifted her head from the hard ground, pounding her fist in frustration. "Go, Ivey . . . *go.* Leave me." She gathered herself as Ivey shot forward across the grassy field. She sat on the ground as a rumble moved the earth, vibrating through her bones.

From out of the ground rose the sides of a sphere.

"Iveeeey!" she screamed.

The giant sphere continued to rise, enclosing the city, enclosing the walls of the Womb, sealing in whatever danger might lurk inside. She felt Ivey's aura, heard her exhilaration.

*"Yeah."* Ivey sailed the sphere over the rising walls, the escort minions flying as fast as their wings would take them.

And in less than a blink of an eye, Daisy was alone. Breathing deeply, she calmed her heaving chest, forced her tears to slow, and prayed to the Womb to save her mother and Peter. She pressed her fingers to her eyes, relieving some of their strain. The field was quiet, the Womb fully encapsulated. She glanced up to see the moonlight that cast her shadow across the grassland. She wondered what could have happened inside the Womb. Shuddering with the knowledge that it could be almost anything, she hugged her body, and felt forlorn and abandoned.

From out of nowhere, she felt a light touch snake around her neck, blowing softly. She held out her hands to receive Tobi's trunk, holding it close and resting her head against it.

"I love you, Tobi," she whispered. From Daisy's neck came a vibration off her cartilage that Tobi received through the pads of her great and sensitive feet. She responded with a rumble, deep in her stomach. Slowly, the rest of the herd gathered round the distraught, childlike wunderkind. In the darkness woman and beast prayed together.

# Twenty Eight Days AE (After Earth)

# Chapter 18

Jose's tongue stuck to the roof of his mouth, his throat dry and raw. He could smell an unidentifiable odor that was making his stomach rebel. *Where am I?* The surface where he was lying was cold and unyielding. He winced as pain erupted from his chest making him spasm, which exacerbated the feeling.

Shaking his head, he tried to clear his sight from the blood that leaked from his facial wound. Looking down, he discovered blood congealing down the front of his bib. Awkwardly, he reached up to remove his contamination apparatus, discovering it was smashed.

He forced himself to his knees after removing his apparatus, rubbing his eyes and moaning. *Holy shit.*

Looking towards the open door to Leeja's enclosure he realized he was in the airlock. He stumbled forward to look inside for her. Gripping the door frame for balance, he peered inside. Empty. He made to go. A flash of darkness caught his gaze. Low . . . on the floor . . . oval. *Maybe she left something on the floor for me.*

Wondering how he was going to find her, he crept toward it. Gingerly he bent down and lifted a surprisingly heavy, egg-shaped object about twelve inches high and with a five-inch circumference. He tapped on the sides and held it up to the light. His scrutiny revealed nothing. But it was hers. He had to hang on to it in case it revealed a clue to her whereabouts and the identity of his assailant.

He dreaded the thought that his assailant may have gotten his hands on her. Secreting the object in the prodigious pocket of his smock, he snapped his tail and turned to leave. In the airlock he was again assaulted by the strange odor. Something like warm carrion; metallic and base. A feeling of horror sobered Jose, his flesh clammy and crawling.

He crept from the airlock to a storage area of silence; nothing new or unusual there. Relaxing but still disturbed by the odor, he wondered how long he'd been unconscious.

Rounding the corner and entering the main room, his stomach dropped like a stone. Disbelieving eyes registered the iridescent blood that spattered the floor and the wet walls. Golden bits of flesh piled at the base of the floorboards; dismembered shining limbs mounded in heaps.

Jose's horror escalated as he slowly took in the pile at the door from the main airlock to the outside. A small form lay at the base of the door, crunched and tossed aside like a discarded doll, suddenly out of favor. He crept forward, his head shaking, eyes dull with shock as he refused to believe what lay before him.

He knelt down and slid his arms under the tiny body of Doodiet, her head hanging by a thread, bright life blood soaking his clothes.

"Noooooo, please." Holding her body in his arms, he staggered back to face the carnage. With dull and glazed eyes, his senses skipped a beat. Try as he may to deny it, he knew the only thing responsible had to be one of the guests housed here in the restricted area. He quickly raised his lion-like tail into the air and opened its bulbous end to release the extruded flesh from inside his tail. The smell of ozone seeped into his nostrils as he directed his healing powers to the lifeless Doodiet. Nothing. Her head lolled limply. He reached down to brace it before it separated from her body completely. Nothing happened. He held her body tightly to his and wept.

The oval object rested heavily in his pocket. What was it and where was Leeja? Praying she was unharmed, he mournfully held Doodiet to his chest, closed his wings over them both, thought of his old bedroom back in the survivors' quarters and disappeared.

The survivors huddled together in Dezi's kitchen, without the lovely ambient light that usually flooded their rooms. The only light was the glow from the eyes of the Elders: Abby, Netty, and Wil. Baby sat with the dogs huddled together on the floor, his arms around Teddy.

Barney whined, Echo was nowhere in sight. Dezi hung his head, slapping his forehead with an impotent hand.

"Why did I let them go? I knew Chloe was in no condition."

Hud reached out to give his shoulder a squeeze. "It's not your fault. Jose is her brother. And Echo and Kenya are with her. They'll get back somehow."

They all glanced involuntarily toward the hall that led to the doorway of their quarters, now shrouded and blocked by a thick, fibrous covering, pliant but indestructible. No one could get in or get out.

Cobby spoke up. "Why do you think they sealed us in here?" He turned to Netty and Wil. "Do you guys know anything?"

Wil shook his head. "I told you, Cobby. We're in the dark as much as you are." He inclined his head toward Baby. "I can't get anything from Baby either. Just that death is afoot. That's good enough for me. I suggest we sit tight and make the best of it. I don't want anyone else put in jeopardy."

Kane began to pace with frustration, giving Cobby tight smiles. "There must be something we can do. You can't expect me to just sit here while my wife is out there with who knows what."

Netty tried to calm him down. "I don't believe the Womb would let any harm come to the girls. And Echo and Caesar are with them. They are quite capable of handling anything that comes their way."

A clatter and thud came from the back of the room where orders were delivered. Kenya's voice was heard screeching. "You are *not* going to *ever* get me to ever, ever ride in that creature again."

Everyone rushed to the back of the room where they saw a house Kreyven disappearing into the Womb's wall while Chloe, Kenya, Echo and Caesar lay sprawled on the floor.

Kenya got to her knees and stood, fluffing her dark mane of curls. She bent over to give Chloe a hand. "You okay, chickey?"

Kane ran up to his wife and threw his arms around her.

She batted her eyes at him.

"I love that you missed me, hon, but we just had one hell of a scare." Her big eyes filled as she described what happened and detailed the monstrous creature. "We need to protect ourselves."

Her face dropped, the blood draining and panic setting in. "The baby. Where's the baby?" She clutched madly at Kane, her eyes wild and head turning to search the room.

Netty put her arm around Chloe. "Relax, ladies. Come over here. The babies are fine. Bonnie's with them and they're sealed in the nursery. They're well-protected. Come on." She motioned to Kane to sit Kenya in a chair. "So tell us more."

Baby and Barney ran to Echo. The two minions touched, heads bowed, fingers clenched.

Before anyone could speak, Echo announced her aura. "It was the trypid—a vicious shape-shifter. It knows only death and cannot exist peacefully with other species. It is loose and thirsty for revenge for her captivity. She knows we have been waiting for her egg. Her time must be near and she wants to find a place to hatch it. I don't know how she got out but there has been much death. We feel it . . . every single one." Echo's aura faltered.

"My Brother Jose has been drawn to the creature. It found us in his room. He must still be in the restricted area. She will be looking for a small safe space to lay her egg and incubate it. We cannot let her hatch out the egg. She must be stopped. My implant may not hold. The trypid does not have a brain like most species. It is a complex system of cells that culminate with an extraordinary nervous system that controls its defenses. It can vanish at will or change shape as it senses thoughts from our brains."

The minions conferred silently, golden eyes glowing in the dark, stoic and solemn. Suddenly a premonition made them look to the hallway where they saw Jose standing, his wings folding back in on his shoulders, a limp body in his arms. Dampness on his cheeks glistened in the glow of his luminous eyes.

"I didn't mean for her to get hurt," he said, his voice a monotone whisper, everyone froze. "She didn't deserve this. I'm so sorry." He looked up from his burden, to see condemnation in their faces.

"What have you *done,* Jose?" Netty spoke low and softly as she edged her way over and lifted Doodiet's body from his arms. She whimpered pitifully as she discovered who it was. Clutching the small form to her chest like a child, Doodiet's head hung alarmingly from the rest of her body. Netty called for Wil, tears now dropping.

Together they took Doodiet into a bedroom as the rest watched spellbound. Jose held out his hand then dropped it to his side uselessly. "I need to find Leeja," he whispered with a whimper.

Baby and Echo trundled after them, mute and visibly distraught. They turned back to Jose.

Chloe's voice rang out. "Jose, who is Leeja?"

Jose cracked a shy smile. "She's someone I met in the restricted area. She's human. You can imagine my surprise when I found another human housed there."

Kenya's voice was firm. "What do you mean *housed,* Jose? Is she a specimen? Part of a study?" Kenya's voice rose to a screech. "Was she in a cage?" Kenya rose from her chair. She marched over to Jose who stood dumbly. *"Answer me."* She slapped him across the face. "Answer me, you fool!" Her voice broke as Kane pulled her back and held her close, her tears bringing her close to hysteria. Cobby opened his mouth to speak and was silenced by Abby with a quick look and shake of her head.

Slipping over to Jose, Abby explained the little they knew, concluding with the beast Chloe and Kenya had encountered in his room and the information relayed by Echo down to the facts about the creature's egg. Jose looked green, his eyes guilty.

Cobby finally stood up, his tone bitter and angry. "What is it, Jose? What else have you done?"

Jose ignored Cobby, addressing Abby, his pleading tone begging her to understand. "I just wanted to give her a treat. Dezi had so much left from Daisy's aborted welcome home party. I just opened the door from the airlock a crack when someone attacked me. I was out for such a long time. I think they got her . . . Leeja. When I came to, she was gone." His face crumbled and cratered. "All of the minions . . . so many . . . so much blood and carnage." His eyes flew back and forth looking for support, spittle flying from his lips. "It was an accident*.*"

Dezi could take no more. "An accident? Are you kidding us? The babe you have the hots for is one nasty number. Some kind of shape-shifter. With a mug even its mother would refuse to kiss, 'cause it would chew her face off!"

Silence descended after Dezi's outburst, all eyes on Jose.

"An egg you said, Abby?" Jose's voice faltered, his expression wooden and stiff. "Are you sure?"

"Yes, I'm sure. What? Do you know something about this, Jose?" Abby's tone had an edge. The rest of the survivors emanated anger and icy demeanors.

Jose appealed to Wil. "Come on, bro. You believe it was an accident don't you?"

"You let the trypid control you, Jose." Wil's voice rang low and tight, solidifying the consensuses. "I don't know how long we'll be shut up in here. We're worried about Bonnie and the babies. Thank the Womb that the trypid will be busy looking for a place to lay her egg. They will be able to contain her there."

Jose turned ashen. "Ah . . . well . . . what if her egg has already been laid?"

Netty and Wil exchanged worrisome glances.

Abby rose from her seat and walked toward him as if a trance. "What's in your pockets, Jose?" Her voice was innocent and light. Yet a high-strung note of steel betrayed her intent. "Well, Jose?"

He leaned from foot to foot, indecision and guilt sitting repellently on his face. The room was silent as breath was held by all; each survivor awaiting his answer.

Abby reached out her hand and pushed him. "Show me. We want to see. Tell us you didn't." Her voice rose, loud with a frenetic note. "You didn't risk all our lives for your own selfish desire."

Jose recoiled, his face pale and drained. "Abby, no. Don't say that. I would never . . ."

Wil strode up to join Abby, confounding Jose with his steady gaze. "Et tu, Brute? I never expected *you* to turn on me, Wil."

Wil remained stoic. "Let's just have a look, shall we, Jose?" He reached toward Jose's pocket as Jose slapped his arm away, defiance proclaiming his guilt.

"*It's mine.*" Seconds ticked away at his declaration. He finally reached into his voluminous pocket and withdrew the object. The trypid's egg in all its soon-to-hatch glory. Abby recoiled.

Kenya and Chloe screamed. "No, Jose. You didn't!"

"Get that effing thing outa here!"

Suddenly Echo's aura intruded. "You must leave right now, Brother Jose. She will find her egg. We are all in danger. My minion Brothers and Sisters are dying as she looks. It will not be long. The Womb protects us now but you must go. You must."

All eyes bore into his, their messages of terror, disappointment, revulsion and panic loud and clear. He turned again to Abby. "But Abby . . ."

Abby blinked slowly, her wings trembled. She turned her back to him and walked away to slip her arm through Cobby's and face Jose, her glowing eyes hard enough to turn water to stone.

"There is nothing more to say, Jose. Just get that thing out of here."

He opened his mouth to speak, then closed it when his eyes lit on Chloe, her tears flowing in anguish, her loyalty to her baby clear as she cupped her abdomen. Kenya's eyes flashed at him, alternating between fire and fear. Dezi and Cobby showed only disdain, Wil was stoic but resolute. Netty was the only unreadable face. Even Baby and Echo, who had returned, held their heads in sorrow.

Not a glimmer of hope or support from anyone. Jose was filled with shame and despair, his regret a knife blade to his soul. He raised his wings, wrapped them around himself and disappeared, still holding the trypid egg.

# Chapter 19

The rescue team stood in front of the entrance to the Healer, the Womb's membrane taut across the opening.

Ivey approached the wall and reached through the membrane. Nothing happened. She glanced back at the bodies of the man and the woman. She knew they didn't have long. The only chance they had was to get inside the Healer. And fast.

They were now completely aware of the trypid on the loose. Ivey well knew of its insidious talents and lust for blood since she'd been in on the trypid's capture to begin with. She watched her Brothers and Sisters as they fought for a way inside the Healer, the life of the man and woman depending on their ministrations. They periodically glanced her way.

She beckoned with her aura, signaling for them all. "Let us try together."

The golden creatures lined up along the Womb's wall, side by side, and thrust their arms through. After a beat, the wall parted allowing them access. Hurriedly, they moved the sphere through. The wall closed behind them without any thought.

Ivey breathed a sigh of relief. She surveyed the room as several minions came rushing over. They helped remove the man and woman from the sphere, guiding them through a labyrinth of supine creatures from various planets that were healing, most confined, some not. They came to empty platforms and transferred the rescued duo. As the minions stepped back, filaments emerged from the walls and sank into the bodies of the hapless couple. Separate life tubes emerged to imbed itself in their stomachs, fluid already entering their systems.

Ivey approached an attendant minion, her aura hopeful but questioning.

"They will survive, IV Navigator. Observe the color in their skin. The gray of death is at bay."

Ivey relaxed, nodding her head. "They have no idea how lucky they were that they landed on Treops. The Treopians knew just what to do. But if we had been just a day later . . ."

"But what of the death in the Womb, Sister?" asked Ivey, reaching out to the attendant.

The attendant minion's head sagged. "It is grave, great IV Navigator. You must stay here with us until the escaped creature is subdued."

"I understand. I just can't believe the trypid was released by Brother Jose. I prayed the collective minion thoughts were wrong . . . a misunderstanding."

"No, Sister. When have our collective thoughts ever been *wrong?* We must pray to the Womb and hope. Now that we know there is an egg, it will soon be over. She is most vulnerable when she incubates the egg. She will take a victim to feed on while the egg hatches and joins her to feed. The trypid will be recaptured at that time. We must hunker down and wait."

The attendant minion walked away, leaving Ivy alone to watch over the rescued husband of her beloved Sister Bonnie and the woman who had turned out to be Sister Daisy's birth mother. She quivered in anticipation of the joy she would bring to her Bonnie. Her acceptance of Ivey's proposal was now assured.

# Chapter 20

Jose stirred on his filthy bed, the sheets crusted with dried blood and rusty stains, evidence the trypid had been there. His eyes remained shut but his eyeballs moved, twitching in time with the unconscious dream that held him captured. A pervasive malaise of impending doom settled like a smothering viper over his subconscious mind as he fought to awaken.

His eyes popped open with a start. He stared up at the high ceiling as he identified the hard object that poked him in the back. The infernal egg. Sniffing casually, he recoiled from the smells of the dried secretions that decorated his sheets and mingled with his own body odor.

Knowing he should get moving, he strove to formulate a plan. Unfortunately, he was so overwhelmed by his fellow survivors' comments and vitriol that his emotional numbness and self-pity paralyzed him. Even his bitterness toward Abby and Cobby failed to rouse him from his funk. Guilt can be a draining emotion, impossible to shake. He wondered why he should beat himself up. Hadn't *they* rejected him?

Jose closed his eyes. *Guilt.* He tried to block the images of the dead minions. Was it possible that everyone had been correct? That Leeja was really a monster? The innocent minions and Doodiet's limp body continued to haunt him as he curled up in a ball and wallowed in his reeking sheets.

He gave the egg a poke, wondering what he should do with it, but too overwhelmed and emotionally crippled to care. Being ostracized by his fellow survivors had finally taken its toll. Jose felt the temperature in the room rise. It took a few moments but the fact that the odors in the room had strengthened finally registered. It had now become foul and rotten. He glanced toward the door as the light appeared to move.

Realizing he was no longer alone, he slipped out of the bed, his tail wrapped protectively around his chest. He crouched against the wall, the bed between him and the moving light. As he shivered in fright, an image crystalized, allowing him to see the hideous nature of the trypid with all its ferocious teeth and flaming eyes. Eyes that zeroed in on the egg lying on Jose's bed. The trypid screamed, the sound insane and deafening. Her many razor plant-like fibrous vines snaked out to covet the egg while her eyes lit on Jose. The murderous intent was unmistakable. No one stole a trypid egg and lived.

Jose's skin crawled with clammy resignation. Suddenly, he remembered the Beretta. His heart beat wildly, salvation within reach as he slipped his hand under the mattress. He would be a hero now. He would be welcomed back into the fold. Abby would be proud of him. His mind danced with the turn of events. The trypid slithered closer, her mouth working spastically, drops of rusty saliva now splattering Jose's bed.

*Come on, come on, where is it?* As his hand fumbled desperately, the Beretta nowhere to be found, the trypid lowered her reeking head toward Jose, her eyes bright with elation and madness. It raised several of its leafy razor projections over Jose and transformed its face to that of Leeja.

Jose hands fumbled for the Berretta as his brain registered Leeja's face attached to the body of the trypid. Unable to stop himself, he wore the satisfied smile of a man in love as the razor projections pierced his body.

The trypid climbed onto the bed and gathered her tremendous body parts to cuddle the egg. She curled up and snuggled in, burrowing into the mattress. She dragged Jose's inert but alive body into the cocoon of razor greenery around her egg. She watched with glee as minute cracks appeared on the surface of the egg.

Without missing a beat, the creature opened its dripping maw. From deep within she shot out a fibrous filament and shot it deep into Jose's body. Jose writhed in pain as the rusty saliva was pumped into his body through the filaments. The trypid sucked deeply and Jose's liquefied flesh began to drain into her waiting mouth. As the trypid fed, miniature fibrous filaments exploded from the cracks in the eggshell to find their spot on Jose's draining body. Mother and soon-to-be newborn settled in to incubate. The perfect location had been found.

The minion team gathered in the weapons room, suited up in their protective gear. Auras flew around the room, fast and furious. Forbation held up his red staff, his aura urging caution.

"The actions of the humans have brought chaos and death to our planet. We will mourn after the Womb has been secured. The implant reports the beast is down, the egg is hatching. She has found a place to incubate. She may be docile now but the hatchling will alert her. If the trypid thinks her hatchling is being threatened, all of you will be at risk. Try to get the hatchling alive. May the Womb be with you and guide you safely, my Brothers and Sisters."

Chloe and Kenya sat in the back of Dezi's kitchen, listening to the quiet whispers of the rest of the adults. Raw emotions and wild surmising drifted down to meet the ears of the two women.

Echo stroked Chloe's abdomen. Caesar rested uneasily at her feet, alert and watchful. Kenya flexed her foot, making it bounce as she swung it, angry frustration marking time.

"It's been hours, chickey," she whined. "I can't sleep, I can't relax . . . I need to be with my child. What if Bonnie needs help?"

Chloe rolled her eyes. "Just what do you think you'd be able to do if she *is* in danger?"

"I'm not sure. But I'm going nuts with worry just sitting here doing nothing." She ran her fingers through her long curls, winding her shock of hair around her fist and piling it on top of her head only to have it tumble back down, cascading around her shoulders. Her twitching foot picked up its pace.

"I'll die if something happens to the babies. Do you think Bonnie is alone?"

Echo's aura intruded. "She has the company of my Brothers and Sisters. They tend the babies together."

"But the beast . . . the trypid. What if it tries to get *in?*"

"It will not, Sister Kenya." Echo's aura was slow and dark, sadness clearly affecting the minion. "It will be looking for my

Brother Jose and the egg."

"But what if Jose goes near the nursery? He needs to pass it to get out of our end of the complex. Has anyone thought of that? We have no idea where the trypid is. She could be anywhere, including close by. Bonnie is completely in the dark about what's going on. That makes her defenseless." Kenya's eyes grew large, her anxiety fighting its way to the surface.

"No Sister. The nursery minions know everything we do. We have a shared consciousness."

Nonplussed, Kenya nodded. "Right, chickey. I forgot. But it still doesn't make me feel good with that mama monster on the loose." She looked Chloe straight in the eye and whispered, "You know darn well I can't just sit here. I have a plan." She hunkered down on the floor, pulling Echo close and looking up at Chloe. "I know you can't go with me but maybe Echo can. You will, won't you, girl? You'll help me get to the babies?"

Chloe looked impatient. "This better not be one of your hare-brained schemes."

Kenya threw her a withering look. "Have you ever heard me joke about the safety of my child?"

Chloe gave her a contrite grimace. "I'm sorry. I'm just on edge. My brother has been through so much lately and now with everyone against him . . ."

Kenya reached out and squeezed her hand. "I understand, chickey. That's why I have to do something to help. I can't just sit here like a dope."

Echo's aura intruded once again. "Sisters, have you forgotten the means by which Brother Jose left here? That means he didn't go by the nursery. He needed to visualize a place he'd been before. He has never been in the nursery."

Chloe slapped her forehead. "Darn, I forgot, Echo. I bet he went to his new room. He knows the trypid has already been there. It might be the only safe place for him."

"I wouldn't be so sure about that, Sister," cautioned Echo.

Kenya jumped up. "Okay, why don't I go back to Jose's room and look for him? I'll make him leave the stupid egg behind. Then we'll go to the nursery together and check on the babies. He can help Bonnie and me bring them here where we can protect them. Would that make you feel better, Chloe?"

Chloe smiled and held her arms out for a hug. "You're really a good women, Mrs. Kenya Cobby."

The two women embraced and Kenya made ready to go. "Kane will have a fit when he finds out so you better play dumb. I'll be okay with Echo with me."

Echo tugged on her arm. "We will use the pathway the Kreyvens use. It will be safe that way."

*"Wait,"* Chloe shouted. "Take this." From inside her skirt, she withdrew the Beretta and held it out to Kenya. "Make sure the safety's off if you need to fire it."

Kenya looked indignant. "What do ya think I am . . . a dope?" She reached out for the pistol and gingerly shoved it into a pocket. "I won't bother to ask where you got this." She eyed Chloe carefully. "Wish us luck."

Taking Echo's hand, they hurried over to the alcove the Kreyvens used to deliver supplies. The same alcove they'd used when they ran from the trypid in Jose's room. Glancing around to ensure they weren't being watched, they slipped through the Womb's wall and vanished.

"Now what do we do, Echo? I can't see a thing." Kenya held her arms out before her, waving them back and forth to no avail.

"Be patient, my Sister."

Kenya suddenly noticed a pin-prick of light that grew as she looked closer. *"Oh, no you don't.* Not this again." Before she knew it, a house Kreyven appeared, its colorful light display familiar and nauseating to the reluctant heroine.

"It is the only way, Sister. We would not make it without this transport. You do not know how to navigate inside the living Womb. *Here we go!"* The Kreyven's wide jaws opened and plunged down on them.

Kenya righted herself, disoriented and infuriated. The Kreyven traveled quickly and accurately, depositing Echo and Kenya at the wall alongside Jose's bed. The wall opened and the Kreyven took off, leaving Kenya sputtering and incensed as she watched it recede down the Womb's pathway.

"That is the last time I get near that thing."

Echo's aura interrupted her, staccato radiance unable to garner her attention.

"I know, I know . . . I've said it before." Kenya sniffed. "Ewww, the smell in here is awful." She squatted before Echo. "You have to promise me, little dude. No more Kreyven."

"Sister . . . there is danger."

Kenya froze. A few critical seconds passed before she had the courage to stand and turn to face the opening in Jose's wall. Her heart stopped, sweat draining from her pores. She tried to work her voice but her vocal cords had deserted her. She took shallow quick breaths and found herself beginning to hyperventilate as her life flashed in front of her. She prayed to the Womb, promising to be good if it would come save her.

"Back away slowly, Sister."

Kenya couldn't move, her eyes fixated on the monstrosity on the bed just two feet from them. Deep in the mess of the trypid and her egg, she could see Jose. Strange appendages protruded from his body and disappeared down the trypid's mouth. Half of the shell had peeled away from the egg showing a red, writhing, wet mass with the same appendages that were sucking the life from Jose to feed the parasitic newborn.

Kenya screamed as a razor sharp appendage wrapped itself around Echo's leg and jerked the minion off her feet.

"*Echo!*" Kenya managed to catch the end of Echo's foot in her hand. With the other hand, she reached into her pocket and withdrew the Beretta. With her shaking fingers, she rested the gun against her side, fumbling and trying to release the safety. Sweat poured into her eyes, blinding her.

"Oh, come on, damn it. Please, please, please . . ." She groped with the gun, her other hand losing the battle for Echo. As Echo slipped from her grip she reached down with her free hand, took off the safety, aimed the Beretta at the monstrous head and pulled the trigger five times, splashing guts and gore onto her face and down her shirt. Echo dropped to the ground as Kenya turned to the hatchling, the Beretta raised.

A choir of auras hit her dead on. "No, Sister. Stop." A team of suited minions rushed into the room from Jose's doorway. She stood frozen, gloop dripping from her long hair, as they scooped up the remains of the partially hatched egg and the hatchling, and whisked it into a waiting cage.

They clustered around the bed to examine what remained of the trypid and Jose. They separated the two with a hook, dragging the trypid carcass out of the room.

Kenya began to shake, shock setting in. Echo leaned against her leg while the minion team finished their mission and departed with no further words.

"*I want to go home.* Tell Kane I want to go home . . . *please.*" She sank to her knees and gripped Echo. "Take me home . . . please . . . I want to go home." Her last words ended in a shriek as a groan came from the bed. She covered her ears with her hands, ready to flip out.

"Help me." The voice came as a whisper. Kenya's heart stopped once again. She rose slowly to her feet, wiping away tears and wringing her hands. She glanced down at Echo.

"Echo?"

"Please," Jose whispered from the bed.

Echo's aura spiraled. "We must get him to the Healer."

Kenya drew back at the pitiful sight of the formerly glorious Elder now reduced to a shrunken husk of a man, his wings twisted and matted with fluids, his flesh gray and wrinkled, and his eyes colorless, puffy slits.

"I don't know what to *do*, Echo."

"Pick him up, Sister."

Kenya backed away even further. "I can't do *that.*" She bit the back of her hand, fear and terror overwhelming her.

"You *must*, Sister. He is one of you."

Kenya closed her eyes and took a deep breath. "Can't you just heal him, Echo?"

"No Sister. I can create Elders by ignoring our laws but I do not have the power to heal one. Only a female Elder has that power. And it has never been necessary to explain the limitation, until now."

Kenya moved closer to the putrid bed, which was littered with bits of detritus and flesh from the head of the trypid. Kenya shook her hands, trying to find a clean spot to get a grip on Jose. The smell was so nauseating, she was forced to turn away to vomit. She tried again, flicking vomit from her chin. Shutting her eyes she bent over the bed, scooped up the shriveled man, and backed away with him in her arms. Echo parted the wall for her to find the Kreyven waiting for them.

Kenya began to cry. "Thank you . . . *thank you* . . . I will never complain about you again, my friend." She continued to sob as the Kreyven opened its monstrous mouth, swallowed the three of them, and disappeared down the cryptic pathway.

"Hey, sleepyhead. You're awake." Kane hovered over his wife, a wet sponge in one hand and Kenya's hand in his other. He dipped the sponge in a tub of cool, blood-stained water and tenderly blotted her forehead.

"Eww, you sure smell rank, my love."

She reached up to bring his hand down.

"What happened? Where am I?"

He stroked her damp hair, having already removed most of the gore. "It's okay, babe. You're safe now. We're in the Healer. You just fainted after you got here and they hooked Jose up to the tendrils. Your eyes rolled back in your head and down you went." Kane looked around. "We're all here. Echo filled us in." The faces of Chloe, Cobby, Abby, Netty, Echo and Baby popped into view, hovering above her.

Chloe reached down to hug her, tears on her cheeks. "You are my hero. *Thank you so much* . . . you saved my brother, Kenya. Thank you."

"So we made it back in time? Is Jose okay?"

Chloe smiled through her tears, nodding her head with joy. Kane moved away from her face and pointed to a figure near the wall. Jose lay with healing tendrils doing their miracle work, his body already taking on weight as his fluids were replaced and his blood pressure stabilized.

"What's going to happen to him?"

Chloe wiped her face with the back of her hand and responded sadly, "Forbation is calling a Declaration. It's about Jose and sounds serious. He's given us a couple of days to settle things down. He expects everyone to attend. No exceptions. I think it's like a trial or something."

Kenya's eyes grew large, worry forming between her brows. "And what about the babies, Kane? Are they okay?"

He squeezed her hand for reassurance. "The babies are fine. They're surrounded by loving minions. Bonnie is now here with us." Kane put on his stern face. "And if you ever pull anything like that again, I will tan your gorgeous behind. Do you understand?"

Kenya blinked her eyelashes in innocence and reached out her arms for a hug. "I'm so sorry. I didn't mean to scare you. I was just worried about the babies and didn't think it would hurt to stop by Jose's room to check on him for Chloe. I didn't think the trypid . . ."

"Shh . . . I know, babe. It's over and everyone's okay."

"And we have another surprise. Do you feel like standing up? We have a *very* big moment ready to happen."

Kenya looked at all the beaming faces. "Heck, yeah. Kane . . . just give me a hand. I don't want to miss a thing." The group assisted Kane in getting Kenya to her feet. Her gaze locked on Wil who stood grouped with Dezi, Hud, and Bonnie. "What's going on guys?"

Bonnie shook her head. "I don't know, Kenya. As soon as the Womb released the barriers from the doors and we were told it was safe, the three of us were asked to come here. We didn't know you guys were here." She looked at Kenya, "I hear *you've* been busy."

Kenya gave a wan smile. "You could call it that." She glanced back at Kane. "So where are we all going?"

A new aura hit them as the IV Navigator entered the room, her brilliant butterfly casting off trails of sparks and light.

"Ivey, I'm so glad to see you're safe," called Bonnie running up to her and kneeling for a hug. "Where have you been?"

"Hello, my great Sister Bonnie. I have been missing you so much."

Bonnie looked happy but confused. "And where is Daisy? I thought someone said the two of you went on a mission."

"Yes, indeed, my Sister. We have been back for many hours but I was detained from coming to you due to the emergency with the trypid. Come . . . I have something to show you."

The crowd followed Ivey through an archway to an alcove. They saw two figures being tended by minions who glanced their way then backed away from the tendrils that connected to the figures, bringing them nutrition and the special healing and repairing of cells that would be so critical to their recovery.

Bonnie stopped in her tracks, stunned. She screamed and ran toward the figures.

Ginger Mae's consciousness lurked just below the surface, trying to emerge. She fought the process, happy and content, warm and comfortable. Something was different and she fought waking up, refusing to let go of the wonderful new sensations that had become part of her lost memories.

An irritating sound was intruding, forcing her to the surface. A woman was screaming. *Is it me?* The sound terrified her.

"Her eyes are moving."

"She's coming to."

"Give me some room, please." A man's voice. She felt a touch on her shoulder.

"Come on, baby, wake up for me."

*Am I dreaming? That touch . . .* Ginger Mae opened her eye and shrank back in fear as strange faces crowded in on her. She could hear hysterical sobbing in the background. She moistened her lips with her tongue.

"Get her some water."

A cup appeared. Someone lifted her up . . . the man. She drank eagerly. The water tasted like molten gold; precious, sweet and life affirming.

"Easy, babe, easy." The water ran down her chin, soaking her robe. She stopped drinking and looked down.

"Oh my lord . . . What the . . . ?" She began to kick her legs and flail about, trying to rip away the tendrils that brought unknowing miracles to her ravished body.

"No, no. They are to *heal* you," said a musical voice, low and authoritative. Ginger Mae looked up into the glowing eyes of the most beautiful woman she'd ever seen. From her position, she could clearly see wings behind the woman, who now clasped her hands between her own.

"Ginger Mae? Do you remember me?"

A cloudy look of confusion filled Ginger Mae's eyes. "Who are you? Where am I?" She tried to sit up but the man held her down. She moved her head back and forth, the beasts of her terrors nowhere to be seen.

*"Where's Peter? I need to see Peter."*

"He's fine, Mother." The strange child-like figure stood at her feet.

"Mother, this is Netty and Hud." Ginger Mae looked blank. "We saved you, Mother. You're safe now."

"Safe?" she asked faintly. She fumbled under her robe, reaching for her abdomen to check the baby. *What?* Her stomach was flat.

"My baby. *Where's my baby?*" Ginger Mae struggled, hands grabbing and restraining her. *"Peter . . . help me, Peter."*

The woman called Netty gave a signal and called for someone named Echo. One of the golden creatures stepped to her bedside. Before her eyes, she saw its antlers crack open. The creature held out a hand and a red drop fell into its leather hand, from where it promptly flew toward her. She held her hands in front of her face protectively.

A tickle at her ear made her reach to scratch. Her hand stopped in mid-air as she calmed down. She dropped her hand back down to her side.

"My *baby*," she whispered. "Please." The woman named Netty stepped up to the man at her shoulder and asked him to step back. She was joined by the child-like woman and another beautiful winged woman. As they crowded in on her, the golden creature with the butterfly that trailed flames joined them. They all stared down at her.

162

Ginger Mae drew a deep breath, amazed at her new calmness. She decided to address them all.

"I am *very* grateful for your time and trouble. The beasts that had us caged were slowly torturing and killing us. I don't know how much longer we would have lasted. But if you could *please* give me my baby, Peter and I will be on our way."

The looks of the strangers saddened. The creature that wore the fire butterfly reached out and took her hand. She felt a delicate stroking in her mind, followed by gentle words.

"You are mistaken about the beasts. They are Treopians, and are beings of peace and science. It was a great tragedy that your pathway led you to their planet. The chemical makeup of organic human beings is different from theirs, as is their atmosphere. Every time you took a breath, you were breathing cancer-causing elements into your body. The water they gave you to drink was not actual water. There was enough chemical difference to exacerbate your cancer growths. Had they not operated as they did, you would have died quickly."

Ginger Mae was stunned. "But my baby . . ." She searched the faces above her, desperate to read deception. But all she saw was sadness, truth and love. "I . . . but . . . but *why* . . . ? Why did they *cut us?* " she screwed up her face. "And where is *my baby?*"

The minion rhythmically stroked her arm. "Don't you understand, Sister Ginger Mae? You did not *have* a baby. It was just another cancerous growth. Every time they cut you it was to remove a growth to give you a chance to live. When the tumor in your abdomen became large enough for them to detect, it was too late. The tumor was very invasive. They were not familiar enough with your anatomy to do chancy surgery. It is the tendrils that have arrested the growth of any cancerous cell in your body. The tumor is still there but the tendrils, given enough time, will absorb the rest of the cancer and any other metastasizing cells. You will be good as new, your leg included. Peter included." The minion swept her hand toward Peter. Ginger Mae followed the motion of her hands to see a woman weeping over Peter.

"Who is that woman? Get her away . . . please. I don't want anyone to touch him."

The beautiful woman with the wings spoke. "It's okay, Ginger Mae. That's Bonnie. She's just so happy to have him back."

"Now just wait a darn minute. *First* . . . you can *stop* calling me Ginger Mae. My *name* is *Bonnie.* I'm grateful for your help but I don't know what you people are up to."

The man's face came into range, full of emotions she couldn't read. "You don't remember me, babe?" He took her hand and came close. "It's *me . . . Hud.*"

Ginger Mae watched as everyone exchanged meaningful glances with one another. Looks of pity and sadness. One of the beautiful women held up a hand to quiet everyone. "Are you a fairy or something?"

Netty smiled and turned to the others. "If you don't mind, Hud and I will sit with her for a while. She needs a bit of history right now. Please let Wil know I'll be ready in time for Forbation. I think we should all go together." She got nods all around and Ginger Mae watched the rest drift toward Peter and the other woman they called Bonnie.

The man called Hud and the beautiful one called Netty settled in.

"Ginger Mae, I am going to tell you a long story. It will start with my life over two hundred years ago. Listen carefully." She turned her head at an interruption. A slender man with a mustache, a sheaf of papers and a writing instrument in his hand emerged from behind Netty.

"Hi, Ginger Mae. It's me, Dezi. You and I are best friends. Glad you're back." A lonely tear slipped down his handsome face. He wiped it away with his sleeve. "I can't tell you how much it means to have you back." His eyes shifted around shyly. "If you all don't mind . . . I'd like to sit in on Netty's story. I'd like to take a few notes." He looked down in his lap. "I'm not real good at this new gig a mine but I'm getting better every day," he said proudly. He nodded toward Netty. "Okay, I'm ready."

Ginger Mae lay fully relaxed, the tendrils knitting her back together. Working hard on the part of her brain that stored memory, they labored to restore cells destroyed by her brief stay with the Treopians, knowing it was one area that would never be the same.

Netty's melodious voice began and Dezi scribbled away.

"I was only seventeen years old. My loving parents were hardworking farmers. The time was late Prohibition . . .

# Thirty Two Days AE (After Earth)

# Chapter 21

The ceremonial gathering room that formerly held joy and celebration now sat empty and silent. The soaring ceilings had been raped of the fluttering wings of celebratory minions that gathered elsewhere to share their grief and mourning in private. Even the sun dimmed its rays in shame for the carelessness of the Elder Brother Jose.

"You can't be serious, Brother Formation," cried Abby. Forbation eyed her silently and turned away without the dignity of a response.

"As I was saying, you will have four Earth weeks. Your companions will be ready to travel by then. Navigator IV will take you to your new home. I am sorry but we can no longer tolerate the disruption and violence that accompanies humans wherever they go. The Womb hoped it would have been quelled within you but I have become convinced that your species would have benefited all life by a final intervention. It has been one thing after another. Sister Bonnie put Navigator IV's life in danger with the rencet, Brother Jose brought violence to another family member, namely Sister Abby when he struck her, Brother Cobby and Brother Jose took part in a physical brawl with one another. And of course, Sister Doodiet . . . and the rest of our deceased minions."

Forbation's head dipped, overcome with sadness. "I am grieved. Please excuse me for a moment." Forbation's aura turned dull, all light diminished. Moments passed as the silence of the room became suffocating. The survivors were in shock.

"Nonetheless, you are here now and still a problem." He turned and gave a curt bow to Kenya. "Due to the nature of Sister Kenya's sacrifice and exhibition of courage, the Womb will allow each of you to select one category of items to take with you. I suggest you choose wisely, for the planet I have selected for you will be rife with unfamiliar dangers. The planet is larger than Earth and similar. It has two moons, one twice as far away as the other so will have a negligible effect on the planet. It has an even rotation around the sun so you will not be subjected to temperature extremes and you will be able to find plenty of water. The planet's life is rudimentary but you must stay alert." Forbation eyed them all, his gaze withering.

"I will allow questions for the next few minutes. From the Elders only."

Netty and Abby began together.

"Please . . ."

"Do . . ." Abby bowed to Netty who raised her head and assumed an all-business tone.

"Brother, we are all regretful of the chaos and death that any of our actions may have contributed to the events of the last few days. We are grateful for any and all help and hospitality you have extended to us. Is there any way we can appeal to the Womb for forgiveness?"

Forbation raised his red staff and shook it at Netty. "It has been decided. Your species is too dangerous and unpredictable. I am particularly disappointed that the destructive human nature has continued in the Elders. The Womb had great hopes."

"Will the Womb allow Sister Daisy to accompany us?"

"It will be Sister Daisy's decision. She has a destiny and is of great use to us. I implore her to stay but she has until your departure date to consider."

"What of the Earth's wildlife?" Netty indicated them all. "I speak for us all when I request that they be allowed to come with us."

Forbation bowed. "As you wish. They will be ready. That will include every last one of them." Forbation's aura felt ominous.

"Does that include the flamers, Brother?"

"Yes, of course it does."

Netty remained silent over the finality in the aura.

"Come, come, Sister Netty. Will that be all?"

Netty remained speechless and bowed after nodding her head.

"I leave you to your musings. It is time for me to join my kind in their mourning. Good day." Forbation's wings encapsulated him and abruptly, he was gone.

The four weeks passed too quickly, the survivors occupied with their life-dependent choice and the health of Ginger Mae, Peter and Jose.

As each survivor decided what their items would be, they were assigned a minion to escort them through the Womb to collect their choice so it could be packed in bundles fit for a Kreyven to deliver.

The pile of goods was enormous. Cobby chose weapons, some easy to operate, some mysterious and intricate. Wil chose tools. Dezi chose kitchenware, enough to serve a banquet to hundreds. Netty chose books from the stars. Kane chose seeds. Bonnie chose medicine, everything from antibiotics to elephant pumices, to poison antidotes. Kenya chose bedding and Abby chose baby paraphernalia, everything from formula to diapers, to onesies.

Once Ginger Mae and Peter recovered enough to understand their situations, they made their choices, although they needed to be cajoled, their minds not fully grasping the reality of the events. Ginger Mae chose clothing: bright and beautiful fabrics, strong, warm and durable that included two lifetimes' supply of sewing paraphernalia with which to craft them. Peter selected farming equipment that included a supply of 110hp engines.

When Jose recovered enough to speak, he asked Wil to make selections of building material in his stead.

The only one that refused to state her choice was Chloe. No matter what was said to her, she refused.

"But Chloe, we need you to make a choice. We never know what we will need. We can't afford to give up a chance to help our survival. Please . . . you need to help us out here," begged Dezi.

Chloe shook her head, turning away as Dezi made a notation in his ledger. "I'm sorry, but this will be recorded unless you change your mind."

"Do what you need to do, Dezi." Chloe walked away, her figure swaying slowly as she left the room, now heavy with child and overdue delivery.

The day of departure arrived. The survivors stood grouped outside, clustered around a portal. Signs of animal dung and trampled grass reassured them that the animals had preceded them. Most of their new equipment had been already delivered to their destination by the Kreyven.

Jose, Ginger Mae, and Peter huddled together, their health giving them something in common. Over the weeks they had bonded with Jose, a help to all three. Ginger Mae and Peter now sported full heads of hair, and complete body parts. Two more grateful people could not be found on Oolaha.

The acceptance of who they were was coming more reluctantly. Hud and Bonnie leaned on each other through the slow and frustrating process. But they were patient. Time was on their side. The fact that Peter and Ginger Mae were alive and cancer-free was enough to ask for at the moment. They were grateful for the chance to woo their spouses back. They had held private conversation about the apparent closeness their spouses had developed while away but decided to table their feelings on the issue until they had a chance to sort it out with guidance from Netty and Wil. After they settled into their new planet. Kane and Cobby stood watching the Kreyven swallow its last load. Cobby gave it a friendly pat as it turned to disappear through the portal. They had a good hour to kill before it would return for them.

"I'm sure going to miss the big beast. It made our life easier," declared Cobby.

Abby approached the father and son, slipping her arm through Cobby's. "Are you guys ready for this?"

Cobby gave her a wide smile and wrapped Kane into the hug he gave them both. "I'm the luckiest guy in all the galaxies. I have a baby on the way, my son who is my pride and joy, my baby that Karen and I adopted, my gorgeous daughter-in-law Kenya and my first grandchild. Did I forget to mention the love of my life is in my arms and I call her my wife?" he asked, looking deep into Abby's shining, love-struck eyes. "We've been through so much. This is just another blip on our radar. I'm sure it will have its moments." He paused and swallowed. "But we are strong. We're resilient and healthy. And we are *family.*" He laughed. "Do we *dare* to ask for anything else?"

Kenya joined them with the baby in her arms. "I'm ready. I don't know what's ahead but it can't be worse than getting thrown off an entire planet." She wore her indignation well, her shoulders high, her head proud.

"That's our girl," said Cobby.

The rest of the survivors drifted closer, presenting a united front as Forbation approached, red staff in hand. He was alone.

A feeling of grave disappointment shrouded the survivors as they prepared for departure. Chloe scanned the horizon . . . not a single minion or nooglet in sight. Even little Teddy gave a low whine as he squirmed in her arms. Caesar chuffed impatiently, unsettled himself by the lack of minions.

Netty joined Chloe, one of the babies in her arms. She waved to Wil who had his hands full with Maya who was refusing to leave, her tear-streaked face and caterwauling upsetting the rest of the infants as they lay in their safety transport.

"I don't understand where everyone is," said Netty.

Chloe's lips were in a straight line. "They will be here."

Forbation approached. "You are leaving without making a choice, Sister Chloe. That is a grave disappointment. We may not be able to co-exist with you but you are part of us. We wish you nothing but success."

"Thank you, Brother Forbation." Chloe held her head high as the rest of the survivors drifted over. "But I fully intend to make my choice before I leave."

"Look," yelled Dezi, pointing to the horizon. Within seconds the minions converged. Tens of hundreds filled the sky, blocking out the sun to light the dawn with their own glowing beauty.

Touching down next to Forbation stood Echo and Baby, Ivey bringing up the rear. The minions stood reluctantly, their three fire butterflies' glorious flaming sparks belying their wretched demeanors. From out of the portal emerged the Kreyven.

"It is time," pronounced Forbation.

Chloe stepped forward and turned to Forbation. "I'm ready to make my choice. That is the last privilege granted to me by the Womb." Forbation nodded. "I request the presence of the rest of my family."

Forbation's aura slowed. "But everyone is here, Sister." He swept his golden hand toward the crowd of survivors.

"No, not here. *There . . .*" said Chloe as she pointed to the minions. "Baby and Echo. And of course, we can't leave without Ivey."

Forbation stood silent. "You have me there, Sister." He bowed to Baby and Echo who ran to Netty and Barney, their joy clear as a green light, the group cheering. "But you are mistaken if you think I can give you Navigator IV. She is not part of your family."

Chloe smiled as she held out her hand to Ivey. Bonnie wiggled her way to the front of the crowd and knelt down. Ivey jumped to her side. "Last night Bonnie and Ivey were married by Netty. I was a witness. By the laws of our civilization, they are now married."

"But they are both female," sputtered Forbation.

"Yes, they are. And same-gender marriage had a long and storied tradition on Earth. Particularly in the United States where we are from. It was a long-fought-for achievement of our society."

Chloe stepped forward to hold out her hand to Forbation. "I want to thank you for everything you have done for me and my child."

Forbation paused then opened his arms to the pregnant Chloe. His aura caressed her mind. "Caesar was correct. You truly are The One. May you lead you lead your family to prosperity with your wisdom. We will be watching."

The survivors made their way to the sphere that the Kreyven would swallow to ferry them safely to their planet.

Kenya approached the gelatinous mass, her neck back as she shouted to the beast. "I'm going to miss you, big guy."

Forbation hurried forward. "Wait. Allow me to make a gift to your success. The Kreyven will not be returning. He is yours, young lady. May the Kreyven always serve you and your family well."

Kenya turned to thank Forbation, startled by what she saw.

*"Look!"* The rest of the survivors turned at her exclamation. The sky was full of sudden illumination.

From one end of the horizon to the other, fluorescent glittering filled the sky as well as from the tears that slipped from Forbation's remorseful eyes, a tribute to the emotions of the aliens toward the departing humans they so loved.

"Aliens weep, Father?" asked Maya.

"Yes, sweetie, it appears they do," he responded as he wiped away the moisture from his own eyes.

Not a dry eye watched as Chloe's radiant and tear-stained face turned toward the waiting Kreyven.

"It's time."

The One led her family of survivors toward the sphere, one hand on her abdomen, the other resting on the great neck of the magnificent Caesar. The rest of the survivors scrambled after her, excitement mixed with fearfulness but anticipation the most tangible.

Dezi poked his way through the crowd, his journal open, his writing instrument poised. "Chloe, wait. What will we call our new planet?" She turned to wave to the weeping minions for the last time, hope and wisdom shining in her overflowing eyes.

"Home, Dezi. We will call it *Home.*"

The End

# To my readers,

Thank you all for coming on this journey with me. I honestly don't believe this will be the last of the series. It is not easy to say goodbye to these characters who have become real people to me. I spend more time in their world than I do in my own.

As most of you know, the fortunes and success of a series rises and falls on the amount of readers' reviews. The more reviews, the more Amazon will let others know of the books' popularity.

If you have enjoyed the series and wish it success, I would be honored if you would leave me a comment regarding your feelings on amazon.com or the Amazon site of your country.

Thank you so much for sparing the time.

J. K. Accinni

# Coming soon . . . Alli Sun

Fifteen year old bi-racial orphan, Alli Sun doesn't know who her parents are. But she knows she must run from the orphanage she grew up in or face being sold to the highest bidder. She learns to live by her wits on the mean streets of 1930s Charleston, South Carolina, leaving behind her budding romance with eighteen-year-old fellow orphan, Dale.

Then her life changes as she rescues a strange set of pups from the forest who go on to protect her in her efforts to discover who her parents are as they survive on the streets and the lowland, going on to solve the most vexing and sensational murder mystery of their time.